MORE SCIENCE FICTION BY KRISTINE KATHRYN RUSCH

THE DIVING UNIVERSE

Series Reading Order

Diving into the Wreck: A Diving Novel

City of Ruins: A Diving Novel

Becalmed: A Diving Universe Novella

The Application of Hope: A Diving Universe Novella

Boneyards: A Diving Novel

Skirmishes: A Diving Novel

The Runabout: A Diving Novel

The Falls: A Diving Universe Novel

Searching for the Fleet: A Diving Novel

The Spires of Denon: A Diving Universe Novella

The Renegat: A Diving Universe Novel

Escaping Amnthra: A Diving Universe Novella

The Court-Martial of the Renegat Renegades

Thieves: A Diving Novel

Squishy's Teams: A Diving Universe Novel

The Chase: A Diving Novel

Ivory Trees: A Diving Universe Novel

Maelstrom: A Diving Universe Novella

———— ••• ————

THE RETRIEVAL ARTIST SERIES

The Disappeared

Extremes

Consequences

Buried Deep

Paloma

Recovery Man

The Recovery Man's Bargain

Duplicate Effort

The Possession of Paavo Deshin

Anniversary Day

Blowback

A Murder of Clones

Search & Recovery

The Peyti Crisis

Vigilantes

Starbase Human

Masterminds

The Impossibles

The Retrieval Artist

———— ••• ————————

STANDALONE SCIENCE FICTION NOVELS

Alien Influences

Snipers

SCIENCE FICTION COLLECTIONS

Colliding Worlds, Vol. 1

Colliding Worlds, Vol. 2

Colliding Worlds, Vol. 3

Colliding Worlds, Vol. 4

Colliding Worlds, Vol. 5

Colliding Worlds, Vol. 6

STALKING SPACE

A SCIENCE FICTION NOVELLA

KRISTINE KATHRYN RUSCH

WMG
PUBLISHING

CONTENTS

STALKING SPACE

STALKING SPACE

IT FELT like Daniella Obregón had looked forward to the boarding processional for her entire life. She hadn't, of course. She hadn't even known boarding processionals existed until a year ago.

Oh, she'd seen them on old entertainments. The boarding processional was especially popular in starship romances—a tried-and-true genre that had more views than any other. As life got more and more grim, people turned to romance to keep their mind off the grimness— and starship romances made everyone feel like they could take a space cruiser to adventure and escape it all.

But Daniella suspected no one could escape it all.

She knew she couldn't. She was single, but she wasn't beautiful, not in the starship romance kinda way. In fact, she'd let beauty fall by the wayside nearly a decade ago when her looks garnered her all that unwanted attention.

Now she dressed like everyone else—loose blue flight pants that could fold in on themselves if she had to don an environmental suit (which the space cruiser company vowed had never happened in all of their years of running ships); a blousy top made of the same shiny and thin material; and a ballcap with the ship's logo that she got as an extra when she booked the trip. The cap was big enough to accommodate all of her silver and pink hair, which she had tucked inside of it.

She didn't look like everyone else, no matter how hard she tried, but at least she blended in for anyone who was scanning feeds or searching crowds. They'd have to zoom in on her face in order to figure out who, exactly, she was.

The ballcap and the pile of hair that had slipped slightly down her neck prevented anyone from accessing her data dot as well. It was legal in places like ports to access a data dot remotely, but to do so required a clear image of that little hollow place where the skull met the neck.

Having her hair slip like that made the inaccessibility look accidental. If someone challenged her on it, she would claim exhaustion, and a lack of attention as she traveled. She would never fight anyone in authority if they asked what was going on with her data dot, but she also didn't want to be easily trackable.

Being easily trackable had made her suffer enough.

She stood in the center of the cruise line's waiting area. The room felt vast, even though it really wasn't. The ceiling appeared high because it looked like it reached higher than the eye could see.

In actuality, it had a flat floor, with a curved dome above it. The floor was clear, which let in the fake sunlight from the dome, light so bright that it tricked the eye into believing that there was an actual sky above them.

There probably was an actual sky somewhere above the cruise line headquarters, but Daniella hadn't seen the sky coming in, even though she was on edge, looking for anomalies like she always did.

She was an engineer by training, but she had spent years designing cities in faraway places, reviewing plans and making certain that cities conformed to the optimal designs for human comfort. So she knew how to look at edges.

What she saw here confirmed the optical illusion that this place was big. The walls had a slight curve, and were darker along the bottom than they were in the middle. They vanished into that clear bridge across the ceiling, adding to the idea that the ceiling was a window that revealed a sky.

The light helped as well. Golden light on Earth's sunlight spectrum soothed as well as kept passengers awake and alert, so that they would be ready for each and every announcement.

And there were a lot of announcements. Most of them had to do with individual passengers, identified by their ticket number for privacy. The announcements were made verbally, in an old-fashioned male voice that had a slightly clipped accent, just like the voices in those old entertainments.

Passengers also received the announcements privately, of course, through their data dot, but everything on this cruise line was designed to replicate those entertainments, and everything in the entertainments was designed to replicate shipboard travel from an elegant and long-gone period on the vast oceans of Earth.

She had never seen those oceans either, but she was aware of them, just like everyone in her department was aware of them. Earth cultures always built their cities around a water supply, a luxury that the early arrivals on many planets did not have.

Cities had been built differently on the Mother Planet —messy and sloppy and disorganized, but always focused on the best way to use and deliver water.

Here, on the dwarf planet Tiberious, not so much. In fact, the cruise line's headquarters was built on a flat mountaintop far from Grandea, the main city in the habitable zone. From a distance, the headquarters looked like a round ship themselves, one that was so big and reached so high that it was surrounded by clouds.

All of that was another deliberately designed optical illusion, but one that felt appropriate to the trip ahead.

Daniella was looking forward to that trip ahead. She planned on a long sleep, followed by a privately delivered meal, and a lot of relaxation. She was combining business and pleasure: she had to get to the annual Engineering Conference on the space station Belikova, but she had nearly two months' lag before getting there, and she was between projects.

In fact, being between projects was the reason she was going; she needed new and interesting work. She didn't want to go back to the Urban Dwelling Initiative on Lakona, where she was based. She was getting tired. Besides, she had been there long enough. And she had a vague worry that her stalker would eventually figure out where she was.

I'm sure he's found a new focus by now, her boss said when she mentioned it. *Especially after that time in jail.*

Her stalker, whom she hated to think of by name, had made her life a living hell throughout her twenties. He followed her everywhere, determined to make a future with her, whether she wanted one or not.

Finally, he had "accidentally" run into her at the regular staff meeting held at a favorite restaurant. The terrifying encounter had left her bruised, the staff terrified, and made the restaurant consider banning everyone. The security team she had hired discovered that her stalker had illegally accessed her data dot, and that led (finally) to criminal charges, a trial, and jail. He was out now, but siloed, according to the authorities.

She chose to believe them, because otherwise, she would be trapped forever on Lakona. She had started to visit job sites all over the sector, with an eye toward branching out to the New Territories.

She was a bit tentative about it because of the varying privacy laws. Even though everyone in the Exeter Union had received a data dot at birth, each region could regulate how the data was accessed and used.

Hence the conference at Space Station Belikova. She needed a change to her work, and perhaps a job in the New Territories would give her that.

It would be a way to safely experience places outside of Lakona.

The cruise would give her time to think, something she hadn't had in the past ten years. Think and rest and plan for a future that overwork and the stalker crisis had put on hold for much too long.

She had gotten the idea of taking a cruise ship to the New Territories a few years back when a friend had informed her that it was absolutely the best way to travel.

And the best thing? her friend had said. *Cruise lines are bound by law to honor court orders. So make sure all your documents are in order. If you do it right, there's no way you can be on a ship with anyone whom you dislike, let alone someone who stalks and threatens you.*

Her friend had been right. But during those months when Daniella researched those claims, she watched too many entertainments about cruise lines. She also watched promotional vids posted by tourists who had traveled on cruise lines.

All of them said they loved the boarding processional. It was the best way to start the trip, they had said, and it augured well for what was to come.

The boarding processional took place just outside the waiting area. Each passenger had a number randomly assigned upon booking. The numbers did not correspond with the level of the ticket, nor with the quality of the room or how much the traveler spent for their jaunt across the system.

It seemed, sometimes, that the cruise lines thought of everything they could do to protect the privacy of their passengers. That was why so many famous people used this company. They were guaranteed protection from their most rabid fans, a situation that made Daniella's stalker seem like a minor inconvenience.

The only time the famous had to mingle with the others was during the boarding processional, and most of them had private security to protect them as they walked up the boarding bridge to the ship.

The boarding bridge was wide and beautiful, a cousin to that bridge near the ceiling of the waiting area. The boarding bridge was a reinforced dome too, that, according to the promotional material, actually went from the planet-bound headquarters to the ship in space, but the measurements didn't work, at least, not as they were publicized.

Daniella had checked, because she doublechecked everything. The flat mountaintop was not high enough to get out of the dwarf planet's atmosphere, and there was no docking ring outside the dwarf planet's orbit.

From what she could find—and there wasn't a lot due to privacy laws for big corporations—she suspected that the ship had a ground-to-space component, and the docking ring was actually in that make-believe cloud around the mountaintop.

She didn't like not knowing what exactly she was getting into, but she was willing to do it for this trip. She had learned that space travel, no matter how short, always entailed unknowns. And as a person who greatly disliked unknowns, she had a choice: she could become planet-bound somewhere or she could stiffen her spine and force herself to suffer the discomfort to have a slight adventure.

She liked arriving at strange places. She liked seeing the fruits of her labor in particular, visiting cities that she had helped design. Seeing them in person was so much better than seeing them holographically.

She learned things—such as the way that floral gardens smelled in the never-ending breezes of a floating city or the fact that even properly recycled wastewater had a bluish glint if cheaper chemicals were used in the purification process.

Little details like that made her planning better, so that she could make good recommendations for the committees planning everything from a new city to a new subdivision in an older one.

The passengers in the waiting area all clutched jeweled numbers that they would have to turn in at the top of the boarding bridge. The jewels weren't real, of course, but they looked close enough to make the trip seem elegant.

A lot of the passengers worked on the elegance theory too, wearing long dresses that skimmed the top of their thin and impractical shoes or a long-tailed tuxedo that seemed wildly out of place in the waiting area. Several people wore ceremonial robes with geometric designs embroidered on the hems and sleeves; others wore pants and skirts in combination with sleeveless tops that had to be cold, since the temperature here was a tad too chilly for Daniella's tastes. Many wore white facepaint designs that went from the forehead to the chin, and others wore as little as possible to display full body tattoos.

She had thought she would blend in more, but her casual attire made her stand out instead.

Not that she was alone. Several other travelers wore casual clothing. Most of them had the nonchalant expressions of the frequent traveler or of the very wealthy.

She wished she could achieve nonchalance, but all of this was very new to her, and she was enjoying it more than she expected. Languages swirled around her like music; children laughed and ran in circles, only to be corralled by anxious parents; and security stood at almost every single entry point, big tall muscular people standing with arms crossed and tubelike weapons attached to the hips of their uniforms.

They were just the physical manifestation of a security presence. The most effective security came from the tiny cameras that floated nearby like almost-invisible insects, as well as the rounded posts that stood nearly hip high and had a small ball along the top. They looked decorative, but they were not. They were small robotic fighters with enough equipment in their centers to take down any out-of-line passenger in a matter of seconds.

She recognized those posts because she recommended them to all of the people she did designs for. *It was better, she said, to have unobtrusive security on every street corner. Save the obvious security for places where you expect problems.*

If the cruise line followed that plan, then the obvious security—the presence of actual human beings—was just a little bit alarming. She had no idea why anyone would expect problems here.

Although, once the passengers left the waiting area, they had to stand in an actual line, not something people did much anymore, particularly willingly.

But the old entertainments showed the passengers lining up for the boarding processional, so perhaps that was why it was done here.

No one complained. The line was what they had expected. It snaked around the small boarding area, and then evened out—two across—as people walked up the ramp to the boarding bridge.

Actually, the entire bridge was a ramp, but its slope was deliberately slight. She mentally applauded the designer, who apparently had been tasked with making people walk up an incline without complaint.

The boarding bridge curved just a bit, and then, after several yards, vanished into the artificial cloud cover. People went into that voluntarily as well, which was not the average human reaction to any place that disappeared into grayish darkness.

As she reached the edge of the ramp, she found herself beside a woman who might've been elderly. It was hard to tell. The woman's bright blue eyes were not a color that appeared in nature. Her lips were thin, and her nose so sharp that it almost looked like a beak. Her skin was more translucent than pale, and in a few spots, Daniella could see blue veins doing their all-important work beneath the surface.

The woman was halfway between dressed up and dressed down. She wore a blue suit that looked like it had come from one of those Earth paintings of the elegant ocean-crossing vessels. She wore ivory gloves with lace edges that kissed against the hem of her sleeves. She also wore a matching blue pillbox hat with a light blue mesh that covered her forehead and brought out her eyes.

As they rounded the last corner, where it became clear who a person's boarding buddy would be, their gazes met. The maybe-elderly woman looked Daniella up and down, as if assessing her for a job, made a slight harrumph, and looked away.

Daniella shrugged. She didn't care if the woman liked her or not.

They stepped up on the ramp together, following a man in a long dress with a cinched waist that made him look like a triangular stick wearing a top hat. The woman beside him—directly in front of Daniella—wore one of the white ceremonial robes, with long sleeves that almost looked like wings. The sleeves were slit from shoulder to wrist, and only stayed on the arm because of colorless bands that hooked over the skin.

That woman wore a hat as well, a derby hat with a long white brim that, if Daniella wasn't careful, would smack her in the face at the most inappropriate moment.

The woman was chattering to the man in a language that Daniella didn't recognize. She supposed she could access a translation program through her data dot, but she had become a great believer in privacy. She also wasn't that interested in what they had to say to each other. She appreciated the noise of conversation, just not the conversation itself.

As she stepped onto the ramp, she was beginning to regret her choice of clothing. This was one of the few processionals in life that a person could be lucky enough to experience. Most processionals were personal—a wedding, a funeral, a graduation—but few were beautiful and impersonal. Those usually grew into a parade.

There was ceremony to this processional, but it was small. The numbers, the waiting, the formal march forward. She and the woman next to her had to wait at the bottom of the ramp until the lights above the arched doorway turned green.

Only, as Daniella stood there, she realized the lights didn't turn green, as in a gigantic green glow that could blind if stared at directly. Instead, they rippled delicately across the arch, creating an inviting suggestion instead of a command.

Without even discussing it, she and the woman next to her started forward, lifting their right legs in unison, and stepping up the ramp carefully.

From this vantage, she couldn't see the top. Just a golden glow, as if they were walking toward the sun. There was no view from the sides of the ramp either. They were walking through a gray metal tube that actually looked like the boarding bridges used on so many ships that used external docking rings. Some of those bridges were so narrow that Daniella, who was not very tall, would scrape the top of her head on it.

The woman next to her would not be able to wear a hat at all in one of those. But this one was designed like the rest of the headquarters; it was both large and had the illusion of size.

Then the ramp leveled out. The top was flat for two meters or more, and the walls were still gray. Before them was an actual door that was opaque with writing that scrolled across in dozens of languages. She recognized the words from several, all of them the equivalent of "wait."

A tiny clock ticked to the right. It took her a minute to realize that the clock was a countdown clock until the door would open.

She wondered where the golden glow she had seen as she climbed up the ramp had come from. There was nothing in front of her that indicated this part of the boarding bridge would open to the sky or the outdoors or the sun.

That golden light had to have been artificial.

She turned ever so slightly, and saw the rigging for the light. The light show was off right now, because it was only directed downward on the ramp.

There had to be—and there probably were—better ways to get to the boarding bridge. Stairs would have been the most analog way to do it, but there could have been an elevator as there was in so many docking rings she had traveled along.

The ramp felt old school. It had also made her feel like she had embarked on an important journey.

She turned her attention back to the door, thinking that the wait was just a tad too long. And as she had that thought, the door slid up with a slight whoosh. The whoosh was mechanically unnecessary; it had to be there for the waiting people, in case they had gotten distracted.

The slide wasn't as slow as she would have thought. The door moved quickly, revealing a wider path ahead of her, with a gray carpet runner that matched the gray on the walls of the ramp.

The walls and the ceiling were clear, as was part of the floor. Apparently the runner was there for people who were uneasy with being above ground in a clear tube.

It made her nervous, which she hadn't expected.

Once again, she and the woman beside her stepped into the new space together, almost as if their movements had been programmed. They hadn't. It was probably something in the ceremony of the doors that encouraged movement at that exact point.

The view came into focus with that step. They were above the flat part of the mountain. Only the rock wasn't flat. It had curves and jagged edges, dips and slight rises that were visible even from this distance.

And for once, Daniella didn't even try to guess distance. She just moved, as she was expected to do, but as slowly as she possibly could. The view was that spectacular.

The mountaintop extended before her, almost like a net that could catch her if the bottom fell out of the boarding bridge. On either side, though, the view extended for what seemed like forever.

On her side of the bridge, the left side, she could see

more mountains, rising like gray broken teeth along the outside of a mouth. Valleys ran between the mountains, some with blue water threading their way through it, but too narrow to accommodate a city, and others with the greens and yellows that indicated some kind of vegetation.

The farther away the valleys got, the more the colors blurred. The gray mountains slid into the darker blue-gray of what she could only assume was water. In the valleys without obvious water, the green and yellow vegetation looked like paint spatter along the bottom edge of stone-gray mountains.

And finally, at the very edge of her vision, the horizon glistened, with just a hint of brownish gold.

Apparently, she had been waiting long enough that the day was ending, because here, on Tiberious, the brown in the gold indicated sunset.

Beside Daniella, the woman let out a small *oooo* of pleasure, surprise, or both. Daniella couldn't guarantee that she had been silent when she had been confronted with this view either.

It was worth the wait. And it shut off the analytical part of her brain for just a moment. As the analysis started to come back, she mentally shoved it aside so that she could just enjoy what she was seeing.

She glanced to the right side.

The city of Grandea was sprawled in a flat valley that also had some green and yellow, but no watery blue. Beyond that, fewer mountains. They were shorter than this mountain range, shorter than the mountains on Daniella's side of the bridge as well.

Beyond them, something flat and brown that looked almost menacing. It almost looked like a dry spot in a meadow full of grass.

Something about that alarmed her and she looked away.

Away meant ahead, and ahead, there were actual people. They meandered forward, far enough away that Daniella could judge them only by their clothing. The woman in the white dress paraded in front of her, and her triangular companion kept one hand on his top hat, as if he expected it to fly off.

The woman next to her had slowed just a little. She was looking down, a hand braced on the clear wall beside her, almost like she expected to fall.

They had been instructed not to stop, to remember that this was a *procession*, not a viewing party. Daniella was about to remind her of that when the woman grunted, like people sometimes did when they got a message through their data dot.

Her hand came down, leaving prints on the surface, and she started forward again.

Daniella glanced at the handprint, watched as the bridge's surface cleared it, as if the print were made of ice.

They thought of everything here.

Ahead, there was a bit of grayish white forming over the top of the bridge. That had to be the fake clouds. There was no way this bridge would take them into space. It felt too solid for that, and it was much too short. The clouds were the kind of illusion she had suspected all along.

And the way the bridge was lit, it looked like they were going to head into a tunnel made of cloud, something that would seem, to the untrained eye, like stepping into the sky.

She was disappointed. It felt like the procession had just begun and it was nearly over.

Then the bridge bounced—a hard bounce, like something heavy had fallen onto a trampoline. The floor went down, deeper than Daniella expected, and hung there for maybe a half a second, long enough for her to realize she was going up whether she wanted to or not.

She put a hand over her head, keeping the elbow bent so that nothing would break. If she could, she would have jumped forward, but from what she could see, the entire bridge bounced downward.

The woman ahead of her lost control of her train and stumbled to one side. The man reached for something— that side of his body lost in what looked like a lump along the floor.

The lump wasn't a lump. A wave was running through the floor—a wave of something—what, Daniella couldn't tell.

All of those thoughts went through her head in that instant, and then the woman next to her squealed as she tumbled off her shoes. She probably twisted an ankle, maybe even broke something. She was reaching for the wall or the floor or something to hold onto when the wave hit.

Daniella knew what it looked like from the outside—almost like someone snapped a blanket over a bed and then let the blanket drift down.

Only this bridge wouldn't drift. It would twist and snap and come apart.

Somehow Daniella kept her footing, knees bent, body centered, knowing that she was going to be snapped upward at any moment.

The key was to protect her head, and she wasn't entirely sure how to do that, particularly if the woman beside her stumbled into her. Daniella kept an eye on her, on the floor ahead, on the walls—and wow, was she grateful that they were near the mountain. The air might be thin here, but there was air, so if the boarding bridge's windows or sides leaked, at least she would still be able to breathe.

It was the little things.

She almost smiled at herself—an engineering smile, practical, always practical. Because if she wasn't practical, then she would lose everything.

The wave hit her part of the bridge, and she rose up, riding it as if she were surfing without a board. She imagined her feet stuck to the ground like some kind of glue. Now, she wished she was wearing her gravity boots, but they were probably already in her room, waiting for her to arrive.

The thought of her room caught her, but she willed it away. The wave crested without releasing her to the ceiling. Her walking companion, though, flailed upward, rolling to one side in mid-air and then slamming on her side against the exterior wall.

The view was tilted, so that it looked like she had hit against the flat part of the mountain floor, rather than against the wall itself.

She wasn't screaming exactly. It was more like she was keening, a kind of grieving and pain-filled wail like Daniella had never heard before.

The people ahead of her hadn't screamed at all, and she had no idea if anyone was behind her.

The bridge itself was groaning precariously. She hoped that was all she would hear, because sometimes structures groaned, even when they were being used properly. But if something shattered—

And then, as if she had willed it with that thought, the sound of breaking glass echoed from somewhere around her. Breaking, tinkling, and then wind, blowing through hard enough to whistle.

She flung herself onto the floor, and grabbed onto the edge of the carpet. It hadn't come off the floor—not yet anyway—but she figured if it did, she would at least be clinging to something that might hold her weight for at least a moment.

Fabric didn't shatter. Fabric didn't break. Fabric could be twisted.

She had to rely on that.

Ahead of her, actual screaming started along with cries for help. It wounded like more than one voice was yelling, and then she thought she heard some kind of announcement.

She couldn't tell if it was on an overhead speaker or inside her data dot. She couldn't really tell anything at the moment. The wind was gusting now, so hard she couldn't really hear anything, not even her own heartbeat.

The fabric and its mesh lower layer was digging into her hands, and something whapped her on the back. She didn't look up to see what it was. The woman she had been walking with wasn't yelling, and she didn't seem to be moving, except whatever movement was being caused by the remaining ripples that were vibrating through the flooring.

Finally, even the rippling stopped. The wind was still gusting, but it seemed to be coming from one place.

An automated voice, speaking the same message in every language that Daniella understood, tried to calm everyone down, telling them to remain in position and help would arrive soon.

She doubted that her walking companion could do anything other than remain in position. In front of her, the woman in the long dress scooched along her butt toward the wall, leaning her back against it.

Daniella didn't think putting that kind of weight on it, after all that torquing movement, was the best idea, but she was too far away to make a suggestion.

The man's top hat had flattened. She could see the bottom of his feet, but nothing more. He seemed to be as stunned or unconscious as the woman beside Daniella was.

Daniella rested her cheek against the carpet. It smelled of glue and some kind of industrial strength cleaner, something that would have bothered her in the past but felt soothing now.

Something normal in the middle of the abnormal.

The walls creaked around her. This thing had to be built for wind and breakage, especially if it went from the top of a mountain to some kind of space station or docking ring. Mountain tops were notorious for wind and wind shear.

The bridge was swaying, almost like it had lost a tether somewhere. If it had, then the whole thing might tumble down.

The announcement sounded again, scrolling through all the languages, trying to sound soothing.

There was nothing soothing about this. Daniella clung to that carpet, wishing she could get her arms around it, wishing she could attach herself to it right now.

She lifted her head and looked backwards. The door had closed between the ramp and the bridge—and that was a bad sign. It meant that the problem was behind them, not in front of them.

Unless doors closing like that were standard emergency procedures. Some vulnerable spaces were built that way—and this boarding bridge was a vulnerable space, no matter what the brochures said.

Her urban planning brain kicked into gear at that thought. The boarding bridge was built in a remote area deliberately. She had seen a lot of security, and hadn't thought much of it—and she probably should have.

She hadn't researched the history of Grandea or even the cruise line she was traveling on. She was intent on experiencing the comfort and the romance of it all, rather than following her usual instincts and figuring out what would happen should something go horribly wrong.

She hadn't wanted to think about horribly wrong and now, here she was, in the middle of horribly wrong.

The woman she had walked with still wasn't moving. The bridge was swaying, but the sway seemed to be in time with the whistling wind gusts, instead of an out-of-control rocking that might lead to the entire bridge falling apart.

Daniella lifted her torso off the carpet, keeping her grip on the sides, and her feet wrapped around the edges. She peered at the woman beside her. The woman's hat had slid back toward the door. Her face had blood along the visible side, blood that was dripping onto her neck.

She was going to need help quickly.

They all were.

Daniella wasn't sure if she should crawl to the other woman's aid or if the movement would unbalance the bridge even farther. Daniella had no real medical training. She just knew how to use the devices that were standard in every single room on Lakona.

She hadn't seen those devices since she arrived at the cruise line headquarters.

Different cities. Different governments. Different laws.

A buzzing caught her ear. It combined with the whistling wind. Something cracked behind her, and the sound of shattering filled the bridge.

She should have laid back down, but she couldn't help herself: she turned. A yellowish-gold circle was forming around the shattered opening. Another yellowish-gold circle was forming a few meters from her feet. The bright light hurt her eyes, made them tear up.

Something—someone—was trying to get in. She hoped they knew what they were doing. They didn't need to unbalance this bridge any more than it already was.

She leaned over the side of the carpet where the clear flooring was, and saw that some kind of open skiff floated beneath the bridge. It was a rescue vehicle—she could tell from the gold and green markings—but of a kind she had never seen before.

Its top was open. She recognized the tumble-entry, something that she had always rejected in her designs for buildings. A tumble-entry was an astonishingly simple concept—the person who was trapped at a great height would tumble, preferably roll into a fall—and land on soft material built to absorb the weight and impact.

Then the material would slide them around an edge, and into a safer place, designated by the design of the receiving building.

But this was a mountaintop and there were no buildings. So the receiving part of the tumble-entry had to be into that skiff.

Her heart rate rose rapidly. The skiff's presence meant that whoever was in charge of all of this thought the bridge couldn't be saved.

She had no idea how to communicate with the person in charge, to let them know that she looked like the only person conscious here.

She had to trust that everyone's data dot was working, and the person in charge knew the situation. Even though Daniella had no idea how the unconscious people were going to complete a tumble-entry.

The skiff moved closer and as it did, she realized it wasn't a skiff at all. It was the mountaintop—or what she had thought was the mountaintop. That flat surface wasn't mountain at all. It was human-made, designed for just this sort of occurrence.

She had two contradictory thoughts simultaneously— she was angry that they had built this, because that meant they knew the bridge was unstable . . . and . . . she was pleased they had built this, because they had a solution in case the bridge collapsed.

The bright lights glowed over her, sending sparks of light toward the unconscious couple before her. The floor was vibrating. She was having trouble keeping her grip on the carpet.

Someone had to give them instructions. Someone had to give *her* instructions. She needed instructions.

The wind had stopped whistling. It was now howling in this space, whipping her loose clothing and slapping her hair against her face. The wind was cold, and smelled faintly of hot chemicals, probably from whatever was causing that gold light behind her.

The carpet rolled under her fingers, and she clutched it in tight fists. The trembling became shuddering and then the swaying returned.

Something cracked behind her, and then it cracked again.

She almost closed her eyes, but didn't at the last minute, deciding that she needed to see what was happening, just in case she could do something—something more than she was doing right now, which was just holding on.

A snapping crack, so loud that it hurt her ears, made the entire structure shake—and then the floor dropped out from beneath her.

Daniella jerked, and swung in the air, the carpet bunched up against a wall that was shattering before her eyes. Pieces of the walls fell to the tumble-entry below her, but the floor hadn't really dropped.

It had receded.

It had been built for this.

The woman in front of her slid and fell rapidly, her white dress whipping in the wind, almost looking like wings. A scream echoed but Daniella couldn't tell if that scream had come from the woman or not.

Daniella couldn't catch her own breath. She had wrapped her body around the carpet, but she knew that was temporary. She knew she had to fall too, because the people in charge had given her no choice.

They believed the bridge was unsalvageable, so they destroyed it themselves.

The flattened top hat floated by her, a disk on the wind. She hadn't seen the man fall. She looked down, saw shoes vanish into the surface, but didn't know who the shoes belonged to.

She didn't want to fall. She couldn't release her fingers. She had no idea she was this afraid of heights. Or strange situations. Or whatever this was. She didn't want to move.

She had become *that person*. The one she always had to factor into her own equations, the person who froze instead of reacting logically. The person who got in the way.

The very thought made her furious at herself, but she still couldn't release her hands. She had to concentrate, do it finger by finger until her right hand completely came free.

Then she swung from side to side, the wind twisting her around as if she was a bit of carpet. She moved her legs away from the carpet, and it whipped upwards, the edge of it—ripped off when the floor disappeared—nearly hitting her in the face.

She put up her right hand to protect herself and lost what was left of her hold on that carpet.

She tumbled downward, feet first—not flying like that woman in the white dress. But that woman had been prone when the floor disappeared underneath her, and Daniella had been hanging, feet first, and that was how she fell.

Almost like a rocket herself. She tucked her arms against her side, and hoped to hell she wouldn't plunge through the fabric surface of the tumble-entry.

Engineering brain, engineering brain. She made herself summon her engineering brain.

They had designed the tumble-entry for all kinds of falling objects, going at various speeds, with various parts hitting first. Maybe even broken bits of the bridge, which could cut into the tumble-entry's surface if it hadn't been built right.

She had to trust that it was built right. She kept herself in a long line, but she looked downward, the wind still slapping into her, making her clothes flutter, strands of hair crossing her face. She took a deep breath, knowing she might have the air knocked out of her when she landed, because this fall was taking forever. Forever and ever and ever.

She was only a few meters from landing when she tucked her legs inward and tilted her body back just enough that she wouldn't be a missile heading downward like a knife into the surface. She needed to spread the impact away from her feet, so that if she hit too hard, she wouldn't break legs or something.

She wrapped her arms around her head, protecting her skull and her neck. Her hands were in the back, but her elbows were on top. She didn't want broken arms either. She needed to—

And then she landed.

Her body sank into soft fabric, going deep into the surface, so deep that she couldn't see the mountaintop or the sky or the broken bridge.

She bounced upwards just a bit—the kind of upwards that happened when someone hit something with give rather than something hard and unyielding.

For a brief second, she did see the sky, realizing that the bridge had been higher up than she had even thought it was, and then bounced down yet again.

She didn't hit a bottom. She was wrapped in a cocoon of fabric, molding itself to her body. She could feel some protective pillowing, even as she bounced upwards again, just not as high.

She went down—not as far—and then up—not as far again. The tumble-entry was working off the force of her landing, absorbing it, and easing her into whatever this new reality was.

Then she rolled—not voluntarily—and tumbled into a wide tube that slanted downward. She couldn't right herself—not that she knew which was "right." She didn't know where she was going and she didn't know what would happen when she got there.

She rolled through an opening, and landed on yet another soft surface. This one didn't have as much give. She could feel a bottom.

The area where she had landed was filled with a golden light, and there were shadows. Voices echoed around her, but she didn't understand them.

The area was warm, though, and she realized she had been freezing. The wind had been so cold that the difference in temperature made her cheeks throb and her skin welcome the warmth.

She slowly brought her hands down. She didn't hurt. She expected to hurt. She expected to have the breath knocked out of her. She expected to be injured . . . and none of those things had occurred.

The shadows had resolved themselves into three people. A woman with a narrow face and worried eyes, clutching a medical device in one hand. A man who stood near the chute that Daniella had just tumbled out of. He was broad and solid, with wide shoulders. His face was expressionless, probably deliberately, but something in his energy spoke of sheer terror.

And the final person, thin and dapper, of indeterminate gender, probably deliberately. Face sharp and angled, almost like a knife, but the eyes were kind. This was the only person who seemed approachable, and didn't seem to be upset in any way.

"Can you stand?" the woman asked. She had a thick accent, which meant she wasn't using her native language. Nor was she using some kind of translation device.

Thank you, engineering brain, Daniella thought. Her brain was going to keep her calm by finding slightly irrelevant things, so she wouldn't think about what had just happened, how close she had come to actually dying.

"I think I can stand," Daniella said. She knew that her response meant she had to tumble off the pad she was on and move away from whatever was here.

She suspected she was the last person off that bridge, but she had no idea if that was true, and she wasn't ready to ask, because asking meant she might find out if some of the others had died and she didn't want to know. She didn't want to know if that woman, fluttering down in her beautiful white dress, had died just a few meters in front of Daniella. If the man had gotten fatally injured when he lost his top hat.

The hat was probably still floating in the air. A lot of things probably were. That carpet might still be hanging down, or it might have sheered off.

She didn't know.

The three people were watching her. She pushed

herself up slowly, expecting her back to ache, expecting to discover other injuries.

She didn't—not yet anyway—but she couldn't watch these people watch her. So she made herself focus on the far wall. It was a grayish white, with some kind of panel along the side. Just past the panel was a half-open doorway, and through it, she could hear faint echoes of conversation.

Air was blowing on her. Not hard, not like outside, but as if she was near some kind of heating unit. Warm air, slightly moist. It was soothing.

The woman shifted slightly, as if the fact that it was taking Daniella so long to get up was bothering her.

"Is someone else going to come through there?" Daniella asked, waving her hand toward the entry. And then she realized that it had closed up, making the area where she had entered look like a flat wall.

She was a bit embarrassed by the question now, because, obviously, no one was going to come through, but she wasn't going to take the question back. Maybe the door would open again.

"No," the woman said. "Everyone is accounted for."

That was different than *everyone is fine* or *we rescued all of them* or *don't worry, we've got you*. None of that was said, but no one looked down either, which Daniella might have expected if someone had died.

She put her hands down onto the pad, and almost

yelped. Pain so intense that it ran through her wrists and up her arms almost stopped her.

She brought her hands up and saw that her palms were scraped raw. Blood had pooled in wounds that weren't healed, per se, but were scabbed over.

"What happened?" the woman asked.

Obviously the woman was not a medical professional. A medical professional would have taken Daniella's hands and looked at them, maybe put something on them or done some kind of short laser treatment to make them feel better.

Daniella didn't answer her. Instead, Daniella brought her hands down again, only this time in fists. Making the fists hurt but not as much as touching that pad with her injured palms.

She slid herself forward, then dangled her legs off the pad. The distance to the floor was greater than she had expected. She had to scooch farther forward than she initially thought just to get her legs down.

Then she anchored her feet and stood, somewhat surprised that she had her balance. She had felt off just enough that her balance seemed like a gift rather than something she could have expected to rely on.

She was facing a blank wall, which was gray like the mountain stone. There was a rolled-up pad beneath it. That was another tumble-entry, and either it hadn't been used, or it had reassembled itself before she looked at it.

"Well, you can stand, at least," the woman said, as if she had doubted it. "Let me see your hands."

The woman had no bedside manner, something medical professionals usually had, just confirming that Daniella had been right: these people were just here to receive the tumble-entries. Nothing more.

Daniella extended her hands, and the woman ran the device over them. It sprayed something cool and soothing along the wounds. The pain still radiated up her arms, but she felt a lot better.

"What happened up there?" she asked as the woman continued to run the device over her palms.

This time, the woman was probably assessing the damage, maybe for liability.

"No one knows," the woman said tightly. But she didn't meet Daniella's gaze.

The woman was lying.

"Okay, let your hands drop," the woman said. "Can you walk?"

Daniella almost said, *Of course I can walk*, but she did just tumble god knows how far down, and she wasn't sure of anything.

"Where do you want me?" Daniella asked.

"This way." The third person spoke. Their voice was soothing, warm.

Daniella had to turn just to see what *this way* was. It was the back wall, the one she hadn't seen. That wall was goldish-white, the source of the light. There was an archway, not really a door, although there might have been a door inside the walls.

She was turned around, because of the fall and the rolling tumble, but it seemed to her that the door led in the wrong direction.

"This leads to headquarters?" she asked the third person.

"No," the woman said before the third person could answer. The *no* was curt and sharp, a *this topic is off-limits* response.

"I'll walk with you," the third person said. They started to extend their hand in what might have been an old-fashioned greeting or maybe just a human urge to touch and bolster an injured person.

But the movement stopped midway, and they put their hand down.

"I'm Logan," they said.

"Daniella," she said, although the third person—Logan—probably knew that already.

"Walk with me, Daniella," Logan said. "We'll get you comfortable."

She had no idea what that meant, but she didn't ask. She started to move toward them, but she was wobbly. Her head felt like it had been stuffed with cotton.

She wasn't quite dizzy, but she wasn't stable either.

"Mind if I help?" Logan asked, holding out their hand again.

"Please do," Daniella said.

Logan put a stabling hand on Daniella's back, and reached out with the other hand, keeping it close to her left arm. Together they stepped under the arch.

The air was cooler here. This was an old passage, built under the mountain, maybe for something else. She recognized construction materials that had been out of vogue for almost a century now, bolts and some sustainers that linked the walls to other parts of whatever this structure was. Sustainers worked well, but gave off their own power, which interfered with other equipment.

The fact that they were down here and hadn't been replaced meant that there wasn't much equipment nearby at all.

"Where are we going?" she asked.

"We're going to get you to the ship," Logan said. "With apologies for what just occurred."

"What did occur?" she asked.

Logan looked at her. "We don't know," they said, but it was the kind of *we don't know* that implied that they had an idea, but not confirmation of that idea.

"Is there a reason you can't tell me?" she asked, and managed to keep herself from getting furious: *Don't you think I have the right to know? I almost died up there!*

"We've been asked to let the cruise line make their own statement," Logan said. They were walking slowly, letting Daniella set the pace.

For some reason, that irritated her. She wanted to follow Logan or have guidelines about where they were going. This walking forward without a clear destination was shaking her up more than she expected.

"You're not with the cruise line?" she asked.

Her brain was working slower than usual. It was almost as if the fall had knocked some of the intelligence right out of her head.

"I am not a direct employee, no," Logan said.

"What does that mean?" she asked.

Logan's hand tightened on her back, moving her forward.

"I'm support staff," Logan said. "I work here, on the ground."

She squinched her face just a little, as if that would make her brain work better. It didn't. It didn't seem to help at all. If anything, it made additional bruises announce their presence.

"Have you had problems like this before?" she asked.

"We haven't had problems like this," Logan said, and somehow that sentence made her feel better. Not like this. Meaning they'd had problems before.

This was something else. Something greater? Something lesser?

They seemed to have systems in place. So something expected?

"What can you tell me?" she asked.

"Not much," Logan said. "I can tell you that I'm glad you weren't hurt more seriously."

She looked at Logan then. They were staring straight

ahead, their mouth in a thin line. Their chin was set. They had piercings along the outside of the ear that faced her, filled with earrings that were mostly little jewels. Although the earring that dangled just beneath the earlobe carried the logo of the cruise line.

Support staff, she silently repeated to herself. *Would support staff wear something like that?*

They rounded a corner, and the area opened up and darkened at the same time. They had entered a rectangular space with the high ceilings that seemed to be the trademark of these buildings. A door was propped open to her left, revealing a wide metal stairway. There was also a ladder beside it.

She recognized the construction as standard, designed as a failsafe in case anything that was mechanical or electronic stopped working. She had designed hundreds of these, usually in underground areas or areas where workers and people could get trapped.

That meant that somewhere nearby, there were automated stairs or a flat construction lift or an elevator.

Logan kept their hand on her back for a moment longer, as if bracing her. When Logan seemed assured that she could maintain her balance, they went to the wall, and placed their palm on the surface at eye level.

A door slid open, revealing another box. An elevator, just like she expected, only this one was bigger than most, and it had another door on the other side.

She could tell that from the additional controls that

were on that side. Otherwise the other door wasn't really visible.

Logan turned toward her and held out their hand. She wasn't going to take it. She was going to make it on her own.

She wobbled her way toward them, and considered the hand, then nodded at it. It took too much effort to smile, so she didn't even try.

"Thank you," she said, "but I think I got this."

Still, when she went inside the elevator, she leaned against the wall. Her back ached, but not as much as her hands. Whatever that cool substance had been that the woman had sprayed on her, its anesthetic properties seemed to fade quickly.

"How deep in the mountain are we?" she asked.

Logan pressed their finger on one of the controls. She couldn't see any labels so she still had no idea where they were going. And it didn't bother her as much as it should have, considering how she usually needed to be in control of everything.

"Right now, we're quite deep," Logan said. "But when you arrived, you were just beneath the surface."

She could picture it: she was beneath the actual mountain now, with the craggy peaks and rough edges.

"The part that's under the clouds," she said, her words a bit mushy. She did not like how tired she was, even though she knew this was from the adrenaline spike. She was not going to pass out.

She wouldn't let herself.

She pushed hard against that wall. It vibrated, but kept her upright.

The door slid closed, and the lights dimmed just a little. The engineering part of her brain knew that the dimming was normal; the exhausted and traumatized part of her wondered what the hell was going on.

"Yes, the part that's under the clouds," Logan said.

It was stuffy in here. Either the elevator was designed without a lot of air flow or the vents had become somewhat clogged over the years.

"They're real clouds," Logan said, sounding defensive. "People ask."

"I'm sure they do." She would have cared a few hours ago, but right now, she just wanted to stop moving.

The elevator was going up. If she hadn't been leaning against the wall, she wouldn't have known it was operating at all. The vibration was almost like a low hum.

Logan kept shooting glances at her, trying not to move their head at all. Clearly, Logan was worried. They should be. She probably wasn't as injured as she could have been, but she was already thinking of some kind of lawsuit.

"Your companions said everyone is accounted for," Daniella said. "Are they alive?"

"I don't know." Logan's answer was too quick. "We were assigned to you."

"Me in particular?" Daniella asked.

Logan looked at her. Their eyes were an almost clear

gray, surrounded by long lashes. They were striking, accenting Logan's features. Logan's mouth was a thin line. It almost looked like Logan was going to say something, but then changed their mind.

"We knew who was on the bridge," Logan said. "We knew how you would land."

That felt honest, and a bit surprising, actually.

"We have systems for everything. They just haven't been tested like this before." Then Logan gasped ever so slightly, one of those small tells that people had when they said something they shouldn't have.

"Like what?" Daniella asked. "The bridge collapse?"

Logan sighed and started to answer when the elevator bounced just a little. The vibration against Daniella's back stopped, and the elevator doors opened.

She almost cursed it. She wanted Logan to answer her before they left, and now she knew that Logan wouldn't say a word.

Partly because there were a half dozen people standing in a ring around the elevator. One of them had a wheelchair, the other guarded a gurney.

"We're told you could walk," said the person with the wheelchair. It was an older woman, who wore a gold and green uniform, one that looked like the imagery Daniella had seen in all the brochures for the ship. "But we brought these just in case."

She waved a hand at the wheelchair and the gurney.

Normally, Daniella would walk, but she wasn't sure if that was pride or if it was realistic.

She pushed off the wall, wobbled a little, and then stabilized. She was still woozy, and that chair looked really inviting.

She made her way over to it, and sat down heavily.

"Thank you," she said to the woman.

"No problem," the woman said. "We're taking you to medical to check you out, and then we'll get you to the ship."

Logan had said the same thing, but the word finally registered.

"The ship?" Daniella asked. "The *cruise* ship?"

She figured that the entire trip was called off due to the accident or whatever had happened with the bridge. But no one had told her that. She had just made that assumption on her own.

"Yes." The woman's response was warm, but curt.

Four people started onto the elevator. Logan hadn't moved from the back.

Daniella met Logan's gaze.

"Are you coming?" she asked. The question sounded desperate to her own ears.

Logan gave her a thin smile. "I have duties below."

Then they paused, almost like they were going to say something inappropriate, maybe a habitual *Enjoy your trip!*

Logan's smile faded, and a very real look of concern crossed their face. "Take care of yourself," they said.

Daniella nodded. The four people were lining up on the elevator, taking each corner. One of them touched a panel along the side, and there was a slight hum—a familiar hum, now. The sound of the vibration she had felt earlier.

"You too," she said, with complete sincerity. She had a feeling that Logan was heading into something dark and troubling, but she wasn't sure why she felt that way.

Maybe because she had been unceremoniously dumped out of her planned vacation into the top of a mountain.

The door closed as the woman pulled the wheelchair back, and turned it around. Daniella looked over her shoulder, not wanting to lose sight of Logan.

The doors were closed, though, and the elevator was gone. She would probably never see Logan again, and that thought actually made her feel bereft.

She was a mess, and she couldn't seem to shake that off.

"I can power it on its own," the woman was saying, "but I can't hand control of it over to you without a tutorial. It's very old. So, if you don't mind, I'm just going to push it."

Daniella blinked, trying to focus. She needed to think clearly, and she wasn't doing that yet.

"What?" she asked.

"The chair," the woman said, finishing the turn. Now Daniella faced a wide corridor. It was gray with no windows and no markings at all.

She felt like she was still deep inside the mountain, but if Logan was to be believed—and there was no reason for Logan to lie, was there?—then she was at the top of the mountain, maybe even in some building that was lost in the clouds.

"We don't have far to go," the woman said, "so I'm just going to push the chair. It's built for that."

"Okay," Daniella said, making herself focus. The woman didn't want the chair to operate on its own, which was odd. Daniella had never seen one of these chairs that didn't operate on its own.

The other woman, the one who had been standing near the gurney, was gone, and so was the gurney. Daniella hadn't seen that woman go, but she did know that the woman had not gotten on the elevator.

Daniella had the sense that this area she found herself in was much larger than it looked, but she wasn't thinking clearly enough to figure out what the clues were which showed her that.

Although the corridor that the woman was wheeling her into was bigger than any corridor she had seen so far in this entire complex. The ceiling wasn't arched, but it felt impossibly far away.

Some of that might have been the perspective from

being so low to the ground, which was not something Daniella was used to.

She had the back of her hands resting on the curved armrest, but she didn't look at her palms. They were aching badly now.

The woman was silent, and Daniella did not feel like asking more questions. The only sound in the corridor was the hush of tires on the smooth floor and a slight squeaking from one of the back wheels.

If there were doors, she couldn't see them. If there was an end to the corridor, she couldn't see that either.

And then the woman wheeled her to the right, and into another wide opening—not a door, really, but a space that was built off the corridor. It smelled of antiseptic and hot metal. There were voices ahead of her.

"This is one of them," the woman said to a person that Daniella couldn't see.

"How bad?" asked a male voice.

"Don't know, but I don't like her color. She isn't complaining, and I'm not sure I like that either."

Except that Daniella wasn't a complainer. She would tell them that if she had the energy.

"Over here," the male voice said.

Daniella couldn't really see where "over here" was, but she wasn't trying either. She tilted her head back, resting it on the backrest for the chair, and thought, maybe it was good that she hadn't tried to walk this. It had seemed far, no matter what the woman had said, and

Daniella was so tired. It was probably the adrenaline leaving her body, or maybe some kind of shock.

She should probably tell them. They would want to know what was happening with her, but they had devices. They could figure it out.

She was hearing beeping, and people discussing her, and once or twice, she thought she had heard her name.

Then: "Daniella, can you hear me?" That male voice again.

"Um-hm," she said, not willing to actually open her mouth. Who knew what they would do if she opened her mouth.

"You're in the medical unit," the male voice said. "I'm Doctor . . ."

But she didn't care. She let his voice wash over her until the words made no sense.

Nothing made sense

She supposed she should care about that, but she didn't. She was floating now, resting, feeling happy not to move.

She shouldn't have felt happy, should she? Not with everything that was happening.

So she mentally shushed herself. She wouldn't mention that she was feeling okay.

They'd figure that out in due time. They'd figure it all out, eventually.

—— ••• ——

THERE WAS A SENSE OF MOVEMENT, and her eyes fluttered open. She was upright, more or less, her legs extended in front of her. She was on a reclining chair, and there was a soft pillow under her head. Above her, and on the walls, were medical symbols from all of the different countries and governments that traveled in this part of space.

The room she was in wasn't a room. But she only knew that because there were windows two seats over, long rectangular windows that showed blurred blue and white, with a hint of round objects.

She'd seen a view like that before—this thing was in space. And it clearly wasn't the cruise ship, because whatever she was in had a small protective wall ahead of her (covered with more symbols) and two heads, framed by a cockpit window.

Beeping, voices speaking in numbers, and some hushed tones behind her. The air had that sour tang caused by being recycled. There were at least three other people in this ship/transport/whatever it was—two beside her near the windows, both unconscious, and someone else on her other side.

She didn't look, though. She felt a heavy fatigue, the kind that came from an anesthetic, not from exercise.

She looked down at her hands. They didn't hurt. They

had that pinkish gold glow, the kind that she'd seen a dozen times before when someone had gotten hurt at a job site, and needed a new skin patch.

She'd gotten a new skin patch there, and maybe other places.

She wanted to ask someone about it, but there was no one she could ask. The other patients wouldn't know the answer, and the only other people she saw were the two up in the cockpit.

She didn't want to disturb them, although she probably should disturb them. After all, they were taking her somewhere, and there was nothing in the brochures that mentioned a smaller ship.

Although she did remember something from the contract she had agreed to when she paid her first deposit. Something about substituting vehicles if the situation arose that such a substitution was needed.

Was a substitution needed? That would be odd, wouldn't it?

She frowned, then leaned back. She wasn't as muzzy as she had been in the corridors or talking with Logan, but she still felt not-herself. Normal Daniella would be questioning everything. Normal Daniella never felt that questions and gathering information was too much work.

But this Daniella did.

She closed her eyes, gathering strength, and felt everything change.

—— ••• ——

THINGS HAPPENED that she was and wasn't aware of. She tracked them. She occasionally answered questions.

There was a conversation:

Do you think she can sit upright on her own?

Yes. She'll be fine once she's settled.

She took comfort in that, and felt them move her. Then she got transferred to another chair, a hard one that didn't move.

I don't know, a voice said. *I'm thinking—*

She'll be fine. Just get her out of that semi-conscious state.

Hmmm. She probably should cooperate with that. It sounded important, whatever it was.

And as she had that thought, someone said, "Ms. Obregón? Ms. Obregón? Please wake up. We're here."

The voice sounded automated, but automated voices wouldn't have a tinge of panic, would they?

Daniella assessed how she felt. Less muzzy. Back straight. Feet on the ground. Someone with a firm hand on her shoulder.

"Ms. Obregón? If you don't open your eyes, I'll have to give you something—"

"I'm awake." Her voice was rusty. It felt like she hadn't spoken for a long time, and that unnerved her. How long had she been in that semi-conscious state?

She opened her eyes. She was in the back of some kind of auditorium. It had a shell front, the kind designed for the best possible acoustics. Shell upon shell upon shell, all facing forward.

Maybe a hundred seats sloped down before her, and they were all full. She turned slightly. She was in an aisle seat toward the back. There were dozens of people behind her, all in mobile seats—wheelchairs, floating chairs, a few gurneys that floated as well, and a handful of people behind them, arms folded or resting on the chairs.

She had been in one of those and they had moved her. They thought she wasn't as injured as the people behind her, that she could handle this auditorium chair.

Handle a chair. How badly injured was she?

Her stomach flipped. She wasn't nauseous per se, but she wasn't feeling the best. Almost like she had reached the end of a long illness and now needed to find the strength to recover.

"Oh, good," the voice said. "I was worried we might have to move you to the back."

The voice had come from her left, which was the aisle. She looked over, and as she did, she thought she saw a familiar face near the front. Someone with dark hair, longer than most, who had been looking her way.

Or maybe not. Maybe she was imagining that. Or maybe she just needed the comfort of something—someone—familiar.

But she needed to see the source of the voice, and she

didn't at first. The people in the far aisle were facing forward, and were too far away to speak to her softly.

Then she realized that a youngish man was crouched beside her. He was maybe thirty, old enough to have a little gravitas around his person, even though the crouch was a position most middle-aged folks never tried to achieve.

He had a kit of some kind in his right hand, which rested on his thigh. He was looking up at her, expectantly. His hair was a deep auburn. It made his skin look burnished, as if someone had brushed it ever so slightly with gold. His wide eyes matched the color of his hair, as did his eyelashes and his eyebrows. The entire effect was unnatural, almost like he was some kind of android.

But he couldn't be, since they were outlawed in this region of space.

Although she had no real idea which region she was in. Or how long she had been out.

"I need water," she said. Her voice still croaked. Clearing her throat just hurt. She was truly parched.

"Right." He rose slightly, raised a hand, and snapped his fingers—which she had not expected at all. She thought he would contact someone or use his data dot or some kind of subcutaneous communicator. But snapping fingers? That was odd.

The move was unusual enough that a woman from across the aisle, sitting two rows up, looked over at them and frowned.

A woman, much paler and quite a bit younger, scurried over, apologizing the whole way. The kind of apology that people gave when they thought they were going to get in trouble or when they believed they might lose their job.

She was holding a clear bottle with water inside. She brought the water over, opened the bottle and handed it to the young man.

He took it quickly, without comment, and turned his back on the woman. She stood there for a half a minute, before turning around and walking quickly to the final row of seats.

The relationship seemed strange to Daniella, but then, all of this seemed strange. She focused instead on that bottle.

The youngish man met her gaze, auburn eyes calm and a little cold. Then he handed Daniella the bottle, without the cap.

"Water," he said. That statement should have been unnecessary, but it wasn't. She had asked for water, and he had gotten it for her. But she had moved to a new mental space, one where she didn't trust anyone.

She lifted the bottle to her lips and took a tentative sip. The water was cool and fresh, and did not, as she had expected, taste like the material the bottle was made out of.

Not that she could tell what the bottle was made out of.

She took another sip, her eyes scanning the auditorium. The ceiling was curved just like the shell up front. This entire space was designed for enjoyment, probably music and live theater, not for meetings.

And this was clearly a meeting.

More people were coming in all the time, some on gurneys. Others in floating chairs. Some moving slowly, as if they were hurt.

This was not what she had signed on for.

In order to wrest control back from whatever had taken it from her, she needed strength. So she drank. The water was cool enough that she could feel it work its way down her throat and into her chest.

The strange youngish man still crouched beside her. As she drank, she noted that there were other people crouching beside people in the center aisle. All of them— her youngish man included—wore uniforms that matched the color of the flooring.

The flooring was a gray panel stone, but it was fluted underneath, probably for acoustic reasons. The chair itself was the same color and although part of it was molded to her body, the rest was tilted at unusual angles, something she hadn't ever really felt outside of performance spaces.

She finished half of the water in the bottle, astonished that the bottle held so much. She moved the bottle to her right hand, resting it between her and the surprisingly empty seat beside her. That was when she noticed that her hand did not hurt. Opening it, closing it, clutching it against the cool exterior of the bottle, all of that felt perfectly normal.

Aside from the fatigue that seemed almost familiar, she felt like herself again. The fatigue, and that edge of panic that was forming inside of her.

She had no idea where she was or how she had gotten here. She had no idea what was going on, and she was the kind of person who *always* knew what was going on.

Her only resource, then, was that youngish man. She didn't feel like she could—or even should—just get up and flee. She had no idea where she would be going or what she was going to do when she got there.

He was watching her, but he also seemed to be taking in everything around them. His right hand remained on the side of the row of seats.

"Where are we?" she asked him. At least her voice sounded normal now.

The youngish man looked over at her, which surprised her. She had thought he was watching her more closely.

"We're on *The Stellar Skyline*." He didn't offer any explanation. He seemed to think that she knew what *The Stellar Skyline* was.

It felt familiar, and she had the uncomfortable sensation that her brain was as creaky as her voice had been.

He moved his head slightly, looking away. He was monitoring the area around them.

Protecting her? Or just beside her because she had been injured?

She was going to ask, but first she had to mentally track down that familiar sensation. *The Stellar Skyline* . . .

It clicked into place with a suddenness that almost made her cry out loud.

The Stellar Skyline was the cruise ship she had booked all those months ago. She had done so because the name was prosaic. She had had a choice of three cruise ships that were leaving from the same headquarters on the same day: the other two were named *Celestial Dreamer* and the *Moonlight Mirage*. She hadn't liked those names, thought they might carry their own bad omen.

She didn't like to think of herself as superstitious, but she was when it came to small things. She didn't like the idea of a vacation line that would be considered a *dream* or a *mirage*.

She made herself breathe.

One step at a time. She was on *The Stellar Skyline*, which put this auditorium into its proper place in her head. She remembered the brochures and the vids. The *Skyline* was known for its entertainments, both live and recorded. Every single performance ever done live on the *Skyline* was available to the passengers, in addition to an incredible vid library that spanned back generations.

"I'm going to need to speak to someone in charge," she said, and oh, that sentence felt good. She needed to say it, needed to reclaim her old self.

"Well, we can do that." The youngish man was using one of those tones people used when a customer asked for something unreasonable. "But you're going to have to wait. The people in charge will be speaking to us in just a few minutes, and maybe by that point, your questions will be answered."

"They better be," said a man two seats down. His arms were crossed over his barrel-shaped chest. He had dark hair and darker skin, and eyes that were the color of an ocean at twilight.

She met his gaze, and he nodded at her. His mouth was a thin line, and deep grooves ran from the outside corner of those unusual eyes all the way to the edges of his mouth.

He looked formidable.

Good.

She might need someone formidable in her court.

"That's why we're bringing everyone here," the youngish man said. There was that nervousness in his voice again. The nervousness was the only thing that made Daniella believe that he wasn't some kind of illegal android.

Maybe his strange looks and the woman's too were something mandated by the cruise line.

Daniella had seen stranger things throughout her entire career.

Now, though, she wished she didn't have a seat toward the back. She wanted to be up front, like she usually was in meetings. If she was up front, it would be impossible to ignore her if she had questions.

She knew how to make herself seen. It would just be more difficult from here.

She leaned forward, and was startled to realize that her back didn't ache either. It should have after that fall.

She couldn't tell if she had improved or if someone had simply medicated the pain away. If she was medicated, then she wouldn't be quite as clear headed as she thought she was.

She was going to have to trust that her data dot had recorded all that happened. She had made certain it was set up for full coverage before she left.

If someone tampered with that, then there would be hell to pay.

She half rose in her seat to see if there was another seat closer to the front.

All she could see were rows and rows of heads, but that didn't mean anything. There was an empty seat beside her, so there had to be some farther in.

"What are you doing?" the youngish man said, again with that panic in his voice.

"I want to move closer," Daniella said.

"I-I'm sorry," the youngish man said. "We can't move people right now."

"I already asked," the man two seats away growled. "I'm not real fond of what's going on here."

"Neither am I," Daniella said. "I'm Daniella, by the way."

"Tyree," he said.

"There's an empty seat here," she said. "That way we can speak like normal people."

"No!" the youngish man said. "You've been assigned—"

"Don't mind if I do." Tyree levered himself up. He was tall and broad, with muscles along his arms and his back. His legs barely fit into the space between the edge of the seat and the row ahead.

When he sat down beside her, the entire row of seats dipped. Another spike of panic hit her, along with the thought that everything was going to collapse.

Well, crap, then. She was going to have some trauma from this entire experience and it wasn't over yet.

"What ship are you supposed to be on?" Tyree asked.

"This one," Daniella said, thinking his question a bit odd. "If indeed we're on *The Stellar Skyliner*."

"We *are*," the youngish man said with annoyance. "I *told* you . . ."

"I haven't seen anything but this auditorium, oh, and the docking bay. Most of us came in smaller ships, and a lot of medical ships." Tyree's mouth thinned even more. He looked grim. "Something bad happened."

"Please, don't speculate," the youngish man said. "Answers are coming—"

"Why don't you go annoy someone else?" Tyree growled again. He was good at using a very soft voice to sound threatening.

"I—ah—can't. I'm assigned to you." That settled it.

The youngish man was human. He had just decorated himself—or someone had—very badly.

"Is there food then?" Daniella asked. "Because I don't know how long it's been since I ate."

"We have a few snacks, but I don't know what you're cleared for—"

"Find out," she said. She couldn't do the growl that Tyree could, but she excelled at giving commands.

The youngish man frowned, and then snapped his fingers, which annoyed her.

"Let's not do it that way," she said. "You should find out."

"I'm not supposed to leave this spot," the youngish man said.

"They all seem to be afraid of something," Tyree said softly, "and I can't find out what."

"You got here through a docking bay?" she asked.

"Yeah," he said. "They loaded us all onto some smaller ships and set them careening here, portholes closed, windows shut down, information ports shut off. Something big happened—"

"Good evening!" A cheerful voice resounded in the auditorium. The voice was so close it sounded like it was in the aisle. But it wasn't. That was the sound design.

A man stood on the stage. Daniella had to squint. That man was tall and thin, wearing a black suit of some kind with a long coat that went to the ankles, and boots that even from here she could tell were solid. A white collar graced the edge of the coat, as did white cuffs unfastened and hanging over his hands.

The white reflected the light, and proved that when he dressed that morning, he hadn't planned to be on this stage.

In fact, he was standing a bit too far to the left, not realizing that the lighting had been set up for someone to be in the center of the stage.

"I know this is unusual," he said. "Many of you are frequent travelers with us, and you've never been keel-hauled into an auditorium before."

The brochures had mentioned that there would be a lot of old-time ship lingo, just like in the entertainments. Daniella had thought she would enjoy that.

She had been wrong.

"But many of you are new and some of you have been through a terrible experience." The man's voice shook just a little. "For those of you who don't know, I'm Jeremy DeAngello, the owner of the Enjoyable Cruises. I needed to be the one to talk with you today because we've had a day like no other."

He cleared his throat and the great acoustics made the sound travel in a small wave. He was unusually nervous.

"He's picking his words carefully," Tyree muttered.

"Worried about lawsuits, maybe," Daniella said.

"Then he should have given us all a canned speech, maybe from some kind of robot," Tyree said.

"Unless he believed the human touch was necessary," Daniella said.

The youngish man shushed them. "You need to listen to this," he whispered.

"Some of you . . ." DeAngello shook his head. "Many of you, most of you . . ."

He shook his head again, then lowered it. As he did so, he brought one hand up and rubbed his eyes, a sure sign of tears.

The personal touch had probably been the wrong idea.

A couple of people came out and stood near him. One of them, a woman in her middle years, clapped her hands together and stepped forward. Her hair was a riot of silver curls—the kind of silver found in wall décor, not the kind that nature provided. Her skin had a silver edge, and Daniella wagered that she would have had silver eyelashes and eyebrows, as fake as the coloring on the youngish man beside her.

The woman looked over her shoulder at DeAngello, her face filled with compassion. Then she turned to the crowd.

"I know this is confusing," she said. "You all expected to be on vacation. Some of you are, and you're in the right place, and until just recently, you thought nothing was wrong."

She took a deep breath, and glanced at the small group of people around her. They were mostly supporting DeAngello, almost as if they were holding him up.

"The rest of you have either been through a lot or are on a ship you didn't expect to be on. We're sorry for that. If you were injured . . ."

Daniella frowned, hearing the echo of lawyers in that voice.

Then the woman shook her head.

"I'm sorry," the woman said. "I'm Patrice Maylyka. I'm the CFO of Enjoyable Cruise lines."

Her voice sounded a bit thick, as if just introducing herself made her tear up.

"We suffered . . ." She took a deep breath, then turned and spoke to a man who was as bronze as the youngish man beside Daniella.

"You're right," Maylyka said quietly to the bronze man—probably thinking no one could hear her. "We should have had an automated . . ."

Then someone waved a hand at her to shut her up, and pointed toward the crowd. She bowed her head, sighed, and turned back around.

The crowd was very silent. Hardly anyone moved.

"Sorry," she said.

Daniella slid her gaze sideways at Tyree. He was leaning forward, fingers steepled against his face.

She couldn't have gotten his attention even if she wanted to. He was staring at Maylyka as if she was giving him the secrets of the universe.

"I figured—*we* figured—" And she gestured at DeAngello. "—that you all deserved a human explanation. Which is harder than I thought."

Her voice wavered just a bit. She took a deep breath, and squinched up her face the way that little kids did when they were trying to hold back tears.

"I guess," she said, "it's all right to show you that we're deeply upset by what happened and—"

"What happened?" A woman yelled from behind Daniella. There was frustration in the woman's voice. And fury.

"Yeah!" a man yelled. "You didn't have the right to put us on this ship. You need—"

"Okay. Okay." Maylyka used her hands to pat the air as if she were patting the people on the shoulder. "I get it. We're all upset—"

"We're more than upset, lady!" another man yelled. "We need *answers*, and we need them *now*."

She nodded, then held up a hand, differently this time, as in *Give me a moment*.

Daniella was getting angry too, but she knew where that was coming from. She had been traumatized, and she was unsettled and she had been in pain, and she needed answers. Now, the people around her were growing angry, and she could tumble into that as well.

Anger was an easy emotion. It allowed for action, but it didn't always allow for *sensible* action.

"All right," Maylyka said. "I understand you're confused and scared."

She paused, and for a moment, Daniella thought Maylyka was going to talk about herself again. That would be a disaster.

But Maylyka stood up straighter than she had, as if she was finding reserves in herself. "We will get to your rights and ours and what we did, but I have to tell you this in order. Give me just a minute to explain."

"A minute is all you got, lady," another man yelled, and something in his tone made it sound like a deep threat.

"Let her talk!" another man yelled.

"Quiet!" someone yelled from the side. The word *quiet* echoed around the auditorium—not because of the great sound quality in the place, but because other people were repeating the word.

Maybe Daniella was wrong. Maybe people wanted answers first.

The hush returned to the auditorium.

"Thank you," Maylyka said. "Thank you for allowing me to tell you this."

She raised a hand and moved it sideways, the way people did when they were working off a prompter. Daniella saw the echo of a digital file—just a bit of red, which she knew had to contain some kind of writing.

So, someone had already written something in an official way. DeAngello hadn't been up to reading it, but it looked like Maylyka was.

Maylyka cleared her throat, and said, "The cruise line headquarters just outside of Grandea exploded."

There was an audible gasp in the room.

Maylyka did not look up. Instead, she stared straight ahead, as if the words that only she could see were keeping her grounded.

"The first explosion was small, and we hoped it was just one of those warning things. We have protocol for problems like that and we were following it, thank God. We got almost everyone evacuated, and we think that's why the first explosion was so small so that people could be evacuated, but then the bigger explosion—"

Again her voice—which had been official as she read—got thick with tears. She cleared her throat again.

"The bigger explosion," she said, just a bit louder, "destroyed the entire building. We could only watch."

The words hung there for a moment. Someone said, "We had family in there!"

And then there were small moans, louder shouts, and Maylyka lifted her hands again, making that patting motion. Apparently, she thought it was some kind of command for silence.

"We evacuated all of the civilians," she said. "It's okay. I know that your families are fine."

"I'm not sure we should trust you," one of the men said. It sounded like the same voice that had called her *lady* not that long ago.

"We will work with each of you to confirm this, but I know it for a fact," she said. She was getting stronger now that she was faced with some pushback. Apparently, that allowed her to get out of her head and her own swirling emotions.

Daniella only felt relief. She hadn't let any of her friends travel with her. She hadn't wanted to call attention to herself, and the fact that she had left home. She was sneaking out, she had said to them, so that no one would even think of tracing her.

They understood. They had gone through all of the permutations of her planning when she was dealing with that stalker.

"Your families are fine," Maylyka repeated.

Tyree let out a gusty sigh, but didn't move otherwise. If anything, his steepled fingers were pressing a bit too hard into his face.

"The losses," Maylyka said, and hesitated for just a moment. "The losses are ours. We don't know how many of our people died."

The words hung in the air for a moment. She probably should have said that the losses belonged to the company for clarity's sake, but it seemed like everyone in the auditorium understood.

"We were dealing with a—with a—vast problem," she said. "Fast-moving, something we'd never dealt with before. And most of you aren't familiar with Tiberious or the layout of the entire area or even with Grandea, but it's far enough away that getting help immediately wasn't possible. Not like we needed. So we had to handle it."

She was clearly no longer speaking from the script.

She was talking from her own experience, and that, some-how, was a bit more soothing.

"The boarding bridges," she said, "which some of you were on, collapsed."

Daniella felt a flash of emotion, something that was even more powerful than what she had been experiencing. The sense of wind and cold and falling and that moment when everything switched from a procession that she had planned for into something hideous.

"We have systems for that," Maylyka said. "We always have people manning the tumble-entries during our boarding processions, but we've never had to deal with three boarding bridges collapsing at the same time. Fortu-nately, our procedures only allow a handful of people on the bridges at one time . . ."

She stopped, cleared her throat again, and that, more than anything else, told Daniella that some people on the bridges had not survived.

". . . so we were able to deal with you all. The injuries —" Then she waved her hand, as if shushing herself. "Well, I'll get there."

She straightened again. This time, when she stopped talking, the silence around the auditorium was a live thing, as if each person was absorbing what happened in their own way, and comparing it to their own experiences, just like Daniella was.

"We had no idea what the extent of the crisis was." It was clear that Maylyka was reading again. "We didn't know if there were attacks in Grandea or all over Tiberious—"

"Do you know that now?" one of the men shouted.

"Let me finish," she said.

But Daniella understood why the man wanted to know. The families again. They might have survived the initial attack, but if they had gone to Grandea, and attacks occurred there as well, then something could have happened to them.

There was a slight stirring in the crowd. Maylyka wouldn't be able to hold them much longer.

"Okay, I'm still going through this," Maylyka said. "I know this is taking time to get to the answers that you want, but some of them are buried in the events."

A mutter rose, but no one yelled this time.

"We didn't know what was happening on Tiberious," Maylyka said, "so we could only deal with what we had. And what we had was our complex. The problem was that the destruction of the bridges seriously damaged *The Celestial Dreamer*. We didn't have the ability or the personnel to fix it right away."

A small *oh* echoed from one corner of the auditorium. Daniella couldn't tell if that *oh* came from just one person or several.

"And *The Moonlight Mirage* . . ." Her voice got thick, and she cleared her throat. Again. "It exploded at the same time as the headquarters."

So that was why there were so many people here.

"It—we—we all . . ." Maylyka glanced back at the entire group behind her, then faced the front again. "We all figured that it would be better to leave Tiberious than it was to stay, but we had a responsibility to you all as well."

She made a small sound, almost like an aborted throat clearing. Then she opened her hands, the way that people did when they were having trouble finding the words.

"So, we got you out of there as best we could, and brought you here, to *The Stellar Skyline*. Fortunately, it's our biggest ship, and we weren't full for this trip. So most of you original passengers get to keep the room you booked. The rest of you will get comparable rooms if we have them. We were all going to the same place, so you will get to your destination, but—"

"What about our families?" a woman yelled.

"What if we get attacked on the trip?" another person yelled.

"Can you guarantee our safety?" Someone asked from the front row. "After all, the other ships blew up."

"Only *The Moonlight Mirage*," Maylyka said. And then shook her head as if she couldn't believe she had said that. But she said it quickly enough that maybe, just maybe, it would keep people from panicking here.

Daniella could feel herself starting to panic again. That was the emotion beneath everything for her. Panic, because she was so out of control.

Voices started to rise. A lot of voices.

"But," Maylyka said.

The voices got louder, all shouting something different.

"*But*," Maylyka said, raising her voice to compensate for the shouting.

The voices had become a cacophony now. Daniella could hear voices around her, most of them urging Maylyka to continue or asking everyone to shut up, but she couldn't hear the overall tone.

Or maybe she could. It sounded furiously angry.

"BUT!!" Maylyka yelled so loudly that the voices stopped. Or at least most of them did. There was still a low rumble inside the auditorium.

She waited until the rumble grew softer.

"We did a thorough search of this ship. We found no explosives. As for bringing one of the perpetrators on board, I hope not," she said. "If so, then they are legitimate passengers who paid for their berth."

People glanced at each other, as if they could tell by sight whether or not the person next to them had destroyed ships and the headquarters and their entire lives.

"We have to find this out!" someone yelled.

That hand gesture again. "Please," Maylyka said as she was making it. "Please. Let me finish."

Some of the people crouched in the aisles half stood and made a shushing sound. That was the first time they had participated at all.

"The ship is safe," Maylyka said. "We're going to our original destination. Each of you will have individual conferences with us, and we will work with you all."

One of the people behind her leaned forward and whispered.

"Oh, yes," Maylyka said after a moment if the person had reminded her to say something else. "The important things. Those of you who were injured. You will need to speak to our medical personnel. We used services on one of the starbases for anyone who needed emergency care, and that helped many of you. Some of you will need more, and we will work with that. We brought a few extra people for our team for that."

She glanced around, as if she was looking for them, but she didn't see anyone.

"And," she said after a moment, "if you have medical experience or a license or something, please talk to our cruise director. We could use even more help."

She put her hands together, almost as if she was going to pray. Then she took a deep breath.

"We . . ." she hesitated for a moment, then shook her head. "Um . . ."

It was clear that she had planned on saying something else and changed her mind.

"If you were traveling with someone and you haven't yet been reunited, then you will need to speak to our information desk. Before you do that, however, please go to your berth. Your assignment has been sent to your data dot, and that will get you to those rooms easily. If you're traveling together and have rooms that were in the same place here on this ship, you will find your companion."

She almost gasped the last word, as if she had tried to stop herself from saying it, but couldn't.

That murmur had started again.

"If you were supposed to travel on one of our other two ships and you booked together, then we tried to accommodate you together. Please do not check with the information desk until you've looked at your room. If your data dot has communication features, please use those to reach your traveling companion if that person does not show up at the room."

It all sounded needlessly complicated, and Daniella would have argued that if she had been in charge. But she wasn't. And, she realized, the people running this ship were as traumatized or maybe more traumatized than the people on board.

The people running the ship had lost friends and work companions, not to mention their place of employment.

They were doing the best they could.

"Some of our staff are stationed near a few of you. That staff person will guide you to where you need to go." Maylyka rubbed her hands together and then let them drop. That poor woman was filled with nervous energy.

"This is a mess," Tyree said under his breath.

Daniella didn't even look at him. She knew that he had meant the comment for himself. She would have told him that she agreed with him, but there was no point.

"Please, everyone, let the people in the back and near the doors out first. Then the people in the aisle seats, all of whom will have companions. Then follow in an orderly fashion."

People were standing even as Maylyka spoke. There wasn't going to be any orderly movement at all.

"Remember," Maylyka said. "Rooms first. Then information desk. We are short staffed, so the more you can do to help us . . ."

Her voice got drowned out in the chatter from the passengers. They were all speaking, as if they had something to add to what had happened.

Daniella didn't want to talk with anyone. She was trying to absorb all she had learned.

Somehow, she had tumbled in the explosion and destruction of the bridge, and survived. They had treated her and gotten her here.

That was good—or good enough. But it wasn't going to help her move forward. Her brain almost felt frozen, as if she couldn't process everything all at once.

The youngish man had stood, his hand extended to her. He was shorter than she was, and a little paunchy, which she hadn't noticed before. But now, she felt like she understood him better—understood why there had been a tinge of panic to his voice when she hadn't initially responded.

"Ms. Obregón?" he said. "I'll get you to the medical personnel."

She took his hand. It was cold and clammy even though the auditorium was slightly warm.

People were moving all around her, talking and reaching for the folks who had been crouching in the aisle. The wheelchairs were floating out of the auditorium. The gurneys already seemed to be gone.

The gurneys finally registered: there were people who were so injured that they couldn't stand or sit, but they were conscious enough to hear what Maylyka said.

Did that mean that there were people who were too injured to even come here? People who were still unconscious?

The youngish man moved her into the aisle, pausing as other people swirled around them. She thought she recognized faces, mostly among the people still sitting down. Most were following instructions, although some had muscled their way up front to yell at the people who were still on the stage.

The good acoustics should have meant that she could hear what was being said, but with all the other conversation, it had become a blur.

A hand brushed her back.

She turned, a bit too quickly, so startled that the feeling went all the way to her toes. She had to keep in mind that she was not herself right now.

Tyree stood behind her, even though he hadn't moved from the second chair.

"I hope I see you again," he said.

She bit back a pedantic response: *In theory, we will have a lot of chances to see each other. This cruise is supposed to last a month*, but she didn't. He knew that, and he was being kind—especially now that he knew she was among the injured.

"I hope so too," she said, then turned away from him.

The youngish man held her hand, but put his other hand against her back. Which was not injured—at least as far as she could tell.

Her hand felt normal as well. All of her felt normal except her emotions and her brain, which almost didn't feel like hers.

The youngish man led her through the growing crowd in the aisle. A lot of people were pouring out of their seats in defiance of the instructions. Ahead, she could still see some of the floating chairs leaving the door.

It surprised her that the cruise line had so many floating chairs, but maybe the ship had picked up more at that base.

It made her wonder how much time had gone by. That was one of the few things Maylyka had not said at all.

Daniella was trying to keep herself calm, and she hoped she was succeeding. She was certainly doing better than the people around her, some of whom were already talking about lawsuits. A few others were discussing just how terrified they were, and one couple was having a whisper-fight about the fact that she still thought the ship would blow up and he thought everything was being done.

As Daniella went by them, she was relieved that she was traveling alone. She couldn't imagine having to manage someone else's emotions along with her own.

The youngish man steered her toward one of the side doors, away from the crowd. The door led to a narrow hallway, painted white. It only had a few people, one of whom looked vaguely familiar.

Daniella had an odd memory of surfacing from something that resembled sleep, and seeing that face. Then the face had vanished into the fog of her heavy sleep.

"Ms. Obregón," a woman said, coming out of one of the side rooms, "It's good to see you moving around."

"Thank you," Daniella said.

The woman smiled. "I'm Marnie Sylvenia. I'm your doctor. I came with you from Tiberious."

"Oh," Daniella said, not sure how to respond. This was all so very strange.

The woman was slight; Daniella never thought of doctors as slight. They were always larger-than-life people, people who seemed so sure of themselves, even when they shouldn't have been.

This woman—Dr. Sylvenia—was old enough to have a few lines along her jaw and around her eyes. Obviously, she was one of those people who didn't care about how she looked as she aged.

"Come with me," Dr. Sylvenia said, and held the door open for Daniella.

Then the doctor nodded at the youngish man.

"I appreciate your help," she said a bit coldly. It almost sounded like she didn't appreciate it at all.

But Daniella couldn't dwell on that. She glanced at the youngish man who gave her a sheepish smile.

"I hope you feel better," he said, which was an odd thing to say, she thought, because she hadn't told him she felt badly.

Nonetheless, she said, "Thank you," and allowed herself to be swept into the small room.

The air was colder than it had been in the hallway, and smelled faintly of some kind of cleaning solution. A gurney rested against the wall, and two chairs were beside it, one at the foot and the other along the head. The lighting was as cold as the air, and just a bit sterile, but she recognized the fixtures: they were the kind that could be adjusted to any type of lighting needed.

In fact, to the experienced eye, it was clear that this room was malleable. It could be anything medical that someone wanted it to be. There were even sterilization pipes extending from each wall, the ceiling, and the floor. That meant the room could become surgically clean, if need be.

Equipment blended into the wall, along with wall pockets that either went to other rooms or there was extra storage space between the walls.

The room's entire set-up made Daniella even more nervous than she already was. She hadn't realized just how uncomfortable she had been with having medical procedures done to her without her express permission.

Dr. Sylvenia closed the door.

"How are you feeling?" she asked.

Daniella decided that full honesty was her only choice. "Confused and frightened."

Dr. Sylvenia smiled thinly. "Which is probably the sentiment all over this ship right now."

That felt like a dismissal of Daniella's emotions, which she did not want. She realized, standing here, that she was awake now, she had some information, she knew that everything was different—for everyone, as Dr. Sylvenia said.

So Daniella could either remain a victim of whatever this had been or she could retake control of her own life.

"Look," Daniella said with just a little bit of the anger she was beginning to feel. "I have no idea what happened to me. One moment I was walking across a bridge. The next, I was falling and injured. Then, somehow, I wake on this ship. So, first, I need you to tell me what happened to me. I thought that's why you brought me in here."

"I brought you here to see how well you made it through the last part of the trip and that meeting." Dr. Sylvenia's thin smile had vanished. "My assistants here aren't that experienced, and I wanted to make sure you're all right."

"Well, do that, then," Daniella said.

Dr. Sylvenia inclined her head a little, then the smile

returned. She seemed to use smiles as a bit of a weapon. This one might have been meant as comforting, but Daniella was not finding it that way.

"We're doing it already," Dr. Sylvenia said. "The room constantly scans."

The anger rose again, and Daniella tamped it down. She was going to use it, but she wasn't going to let it overtake her.

"I thought you had to ask my permission for that," Daniella said.

"You're on the ship now," Dr. Sylvenia said. Her smile was gone again. "You signed waivers for just this sort of thing. I can call them up if you like."

Daniella let out a small breath. "No, that's fine."

"And so are you," Dr. Sylvenia said. "You're healing very well."

And that was it. Daniella was vibrating with anger. It took every bit of strength for Daniella to keep her voice calm.

"I don't even know what's wrong with me," she snapped. "So just telling me I'm fine now is not good enough."

Dr. Sylvenia nodded, just a little, as if she understood. "Yes, yes, you're right," she said. "We've been in triage mode for days."

"Days?" Daniella asked. "How much time have I lost?"

"Let's deal with your health first, and then get to the

timeline, shall we?" Dr. Sylvenia said in the kind of doctor speak that Daniella loathed. *Shall we?* was a kind of enforced compliance.

Daniella didn't argue it even though she wanted to. She bobbed a little on her feet, feeling awkward.

Dr. Sylvenia walked to one of the chairs and placed her hands on its back, leaning on it. She was standing near a control panel that was slightly recessed into the wall.

She didn't look at that, though. She kept her gaze on Daniella, and said, "You were not as seriously injured as the people in Tiberious had thought."

Well, that was something. Although "not as seriously injured" wasn't really a descriptor. Or maybe it was. If they thought she was seriously injured, they would have put her on a quicker medical track than someone who had bruises and sprains.

They had been triaging, after all.

"They were worried," Dr. Sylvenia was saying, "about internal injuries and bleeding that their equipment could not find. You passed out on them. Your hands were damaged, and you fell from quite a distance, even though you landed on a tumble-entry. They had no idea what happened to you on that bridge."

"I held on for dear life, that's what happened," Daniella said, working to keep her voice level.

"And somehow you made it. The people around you did not."

An image of the floating top hat crossed Daniella's

brain. She had been so uncertain on that bridge. Everyone else had been dressed up for the procession, ready to enjoy their vacation, and she had thought of it as a lark, a way to get from one point to another.

Daniella had to force herself back to this moment. "And you want to know how I survived?" she asked, unclear about that last bit.

"No," Dr. Sylvenia said. "Well, I don't. I'm sure that the authorities will get to you. They're interviewing everyone, trying to figure out what happened."

Daniella frowned. "Authorities are on the ship?"

Dr. Sylvenia's gaze left hers. It was some kind of tell, something that showed Dr. Sylvenia did not want to discuss this.

Then her gaze came back to Daniella's.

"There's a lot that the people who run this ship want to handle. I'm only supposed to deal with medical issues," Dr. Sylvenia said. "So, that's what I'm doing."

It felt like a rebuke. Maybe it was a rebuke.

"I'm sorry I was so blunt a moment ago," Dr. Sylvenia said. "Did you know the people you were processing with?"

She had slipped into compassion mode. It didn't feel fake, but it didn't feel real either. It was almost like she had found some kind of program that she could operate out of.

"I did not," Daniella said. "I'm traveling alone. I'm heading to a conference, or I was."

It depended on how much time she had lost, on what she needed to be doing, on so many things.

"Well, I suspect you probably still can make the conference," Dr. Sylvenia said. "Let's just continue this from the medical perspective, shall we?"

Daniella nodded, and as she did, she realized they were both scattered. This, whatever it was, had happened to Dr. Sylvenia as well as Daniella, and everyone else on the *Starlight Skyline*.

"From the perspective of the people performing triage," Dr. Sylvenia said, "the fact that you survived and the others did not is an important piece of information. They didn't have the best equipment. They couldn't do what we're doing right now, which is a room-wide scan. They could only work with what they were seeing in front of them."

"Okay," Daniella said, realizing that the explanation was calming her down. That information made sense to her. Of course, they would work with the tools they had. That was all anyone could do.

"So, they realized that whatever had happened up there had been awful."

"Yeah," Daniella breathed.

"They assumed you were a lot more injured than you turned out to be."

That was the second time Dr. Sylvenia had said that.

"Which is why they sent you to me," Dr. Sylvenia said.

Daniella frowned. She hadn't realized that Dr. Sylvenia was some kind of specialist.

"I work on the starbase," she said.

That surprised Daniella. After all, they were both on the *Starlight Skyline* now. Why would a doctor leave the relative safety of a starbase to come here?

"You mean the base near Tiberious?" she asked. "I thought it was unaffiliated with Enjoyable Cruises."

"It is unaffiliated," Dr. Sylvenia said. "But Enjoyable Cruises has offices there, as do many other companies. We have medical staff there because people who go on cruises aren't always healthy. They have medical emergencies because they haven't been tending to their own well-being. Sometimes they personally just aren't compatible with this kind of travel."

"Okay," Daniella said. She threaded her hands together, noting again that they felt fine. She did not glance at the chairs, although she wanted to.

She was tiring.

"The medical staff on Tiberious was overrun," Dr. Sylvenia was saying. "Their triage was complex, but they followed regs. They sent the patients that were seriously injured but not at risk of dying immediately to us."

"Instead of to Grandea?" Daniella asked. Because she would have thought that the city was closer and the safer bet.

Dr. Sylvenia's face shut down, and that fake smile appeared again.

"I wasn't there," she said. "All I know is that patients who could survive the journey were sent to us."

Daniella was beginning to understand this now. Process questions, questions that could be interpreted about what had happened at the headquarters and on those bridges, were not questions that Dr. Sylvenia felt comfortable answering.

"Also," Dr. Sylvenia said, "the patients we saw were the ones who were passengers."

Daniella didn't like the past tense. How many people had died in this attack?

"You were all heading off-planet anyway," she said. "So the people on the ground made sure you were on your way."

"It also solved the problems of the medical waivers," Daniella said. "You knew we had them."

Dr. Sylvenia's eyes sparkled just for a moment, and she looked like a child who had been caught doing something wrong.

"Yes, there's that," she said. "We did what we needed to get you back on your feet."

That sounded ominous, but Daniella knew it wasn't meant that way. They were only talking about medical treatment, after all. Not anything more sinister.

"And," Dr. Sylvenia said quietly, "we knew we could get you to space. We needed people away from headquarters. The attack was a bad one."

"I'm gathering that," Daniella said.

Dr. Sylvenia's fingers gripped the chair back so tightly that her knuckles were changing color.

"I'm not supposed to tell the passengers this," she said, her voice lowering, "but I think you need to know for medical purposes."

She emphasized *medical purposes*.

Daniella didn't move.

"The ships do not dock anywhere near Tiberious." Dr. Sylvenia's voice was even lower. Daniella had to lean forward to hear. "The boarding bridge actually takes passengers—*took* passengers—" Dr. Sylvenia tilted her head a little as she corrected herself. "—to a space yacht, not the big ship. There's nowhere near Tiberious that could handle ships the size of Enjoyable Cruise's line."

Daniella frowned. That revelation wanted to make her look at every bit of documentation Enjoyable Cruises had sent her. They had implied or maybe even said that the boarding would take place from Tiberious.

She almost brought that up, and then stopped herself. No. This was medical. She could deal with those other details later.

"The space yacht," Dr. Sylvenia said, "takes everyone to the larger ship. It's a deliberate illusion, so that you would feel like you were going through a luxury portal, when instead, you were being shuttled to the ship."

Daniella frowned. "That seems like a strange precaution. Were they having threats?"

"Passenger ships have been targets for decades," Dr.

Sylvenia said and then stopped, as if she had said even more that she shouldn't have.

"Targets?" Daniella asked. She knew she was venturing into the non-medical care area again, but she couldn't help herself. That word, *targets,* was a bad one.

If passengers knew about it, they might not book cruises.

She certainly would not have.

"That's all I can say about that." Dr. Sylvenia spoke just a little louder now, clearly going back on script. "I can add that the trip to the cruise ship is usually very smooth. If something goes wrong, though, the yacht diverts temporarily to the starbase to let passengers off. We then deal with them in our office."

Daniella frowned at her, trying to picture all of this. Daniella had to put her engineering brain on it, thinking about the system, the diversions, what she knew about cities and big, gigantic corporate headquarters.

She wasn't as fluent in how big ships worked, except she did know how they were docked, especially planetside.

Apparently, Tiberious didn't have any docking in orbit, or Enjoyable Cruises wouldn't have gone to such lengths to make it seem like the passengers were on the ship when they actually weren't.

"The docking ring is near the starbase," she blurted. "You funnel employees there and back, don't you?"

Dr. Sylvenia's gaze met hers, but Dr. Sylvenia didn't

say anything else. She probably couldn't. She was probably bound by contract.

Then she looked away and put her palm against the wall.

A screen formed near her head. The screen was opaque, blocking a rectangular spot on the wall the length of Daniella's forearm.

Dr. Sylvenia pushed the screen aside with one hand and pulled the other off the controls. Then she faced the screen.

It sent light onto her face, making her look washed out. She suddenly seemed exhausted, or maybe Daniella had just noticed that. The ordeal all of them had been through had to exhaust the medical professionals too.

"Let's talk about you," she said.

Daniella suppressed a sigh, then bucked herself up. She had been afraid of this conversation. Even though Dr. Sylvenia had told Daniella she was in better shape than expected, she still figured there was something seriously wrong.

Dr. Sylvenia checked the screen. It was as if she was checking her notes. Maybe she was.

"You made it to the station quickly." Dr. Sylvenia's tone was businesslike now. All semblance of confidentiality had disappeared. "The shuttle had better scanning equipment than the staff in the tumble-entry had. The shuttle's crew didn't find any internal injuries. You did have some back issues from that landing, but you were able to stand, or so one of the people who got to you at the tumble-entry said."

"That's true," Daniella said. She remembered the back pain, though. It wasn't as strong as the pain in her hands or the muzziness in her brain.

Sometimes, she knew, the body did that, letting the pain from the minor injuries take over when the pain from the major injury would have overwhelmed.

"They stabilized you enough, and kept you under. Your hands worried them, but they didn't have the capability of taking care of them," Dr. Sylvenia said.

Daniella kept her hands threaded, but her grip tightened. She was able to do that, at least—days?—after what had happened.

"I thought they were just rug burns," she said.

Dr. Sylvenia was shaking her head even before Daniella finished speaking. "It was more serious than that. You got bits and pieces of the metal from the bridge under your skin, and it's toxic."

Daniella felt her eyes widen. They used toxic materials on that bridge? How was that allowed to happen? In her designs, she always specified materials, particularly if those materials were going to be anywhere near human beings.

Toxic materials near people on a boarding bridge—especially a bridge that had safeguards like a tumble-entry —were forbidden, at least where she was from.

If someone knew that the bridge could be easily

destroyed while someone was on it (as suggested by the tumble-entry), then it was required to use materials that wouldn't be ingested or cause illness when absorbed.

Dr. Sylvenia must have seen the expression on Daniella's face because the look that Dr. Sylvenia had was foreboding. It was as clear as day that she didn't want to answer another question about this.

"Let's just say this," she said. "The injuries to your hands were getting worse. Even though the staff on the ground had sealed your hands to prevent infection, it wasn't working."

Daniella shuddered in spite of herself. No wonder her hands had hurt like they had.

"I cleaned them up," Dr. Sylvenia said, "and then, to facilitate healing, I decided that laying new skin would be better than trying to regrow from the old. So I did that in my surgery on the space station."

"Okay." It took a moment for that to register. "You didn't do it here?"

"No," Dr. Sylvenia said.

"But you said you worked out of the space station. Why are you on the ship?"

"Well," Dr. Sylvenia said without looking at her. That lying tell. "I had to keep an eye on my patients."

"Not just me," Daniella said.

"Not just you," Dr. Sylvenia said. "I have several."

"And there's no one on the ship that could have done that for you?" Daniella asked.

"I insisted," Dr. Sylvenia said. There were shadows under her eyes that had grown very deep, almost as if the conversation was draining her.

"Because you were afraid that whatever happened on the planet would find its way to the space station," Daniella said.

Dr. Sylvenia raised her head so quickly she almost overbalanced herself. The look on her face was complete surprise. She hadn't expected Daniella to say that.

But Dr. Sylvenia didn't answer that, after all. Instead, she lowered the opaque screen. It kept floating near the chair, but Dr. Sylvenia came over to Daniella's side.

For a moment, Daniella thought Dr. Sylvenia would say something softly, so softly that the technology in the room couldn't pick it up, but she didn't.

Instead, she said in a normal tone, "Let me see your hands."

Daniella separated them. The bones ached because she had been pressing them together so very hard.

She extended them.

Dr. Sylvenia took Daniella's right hand. Dr. Sylvenia's stubby fingers were warm against Daniella's skin. She hadn't realized just how cold she was.

Dr. Sylvenia turned Daniella's hand over, pressing the palm, then the knuckles, then gripping the wrist hard, almost as if feeling for a seam between the skin of the hand and the skin of the arm.

"How does that feel?" Dr. Sylvenia asked.

"Fine," Daniella said. "Normal." Then she reflected on what she was feeling. "A little cold, maybe."

"Cold is something we have to monitor. It indicates blood flow. Right now, we're seeing normal blood flow, but you'll feel the difference before our sensors pick it up."

Dr. Sylvenia let Daniella's right hand drop. It ached where Dr. Sylvenia's fingers had been.

"Let's see the other one," Dr. Sylvenia said as she reached for Daniella's left hand.

Daniella raised it. Oddly, the left hand felt heavier than the right.

Dr. Sylvenia turned it over and then over again. She shook it, almost like it was a chew toy in a dog's mouth, and then she poked at it.

"Does this one feel any different?" Dr. Sylvenia asked.

"Heavier," Daniella said. "But warmer."

"Hmm." Dr. Sylvenia poked a little more. Then she held Daniella's hand out, clearly doing that for the sensors.

Finally, Dr. Sylvenia let the hand drop.

"This hand was injured worse than the other," she said. "We're going to have to monitor it for infection. I'm not sure we got it all."

"What is the toxic substance that you mentioned?" Daniella asked.

Dr. Sylvenia kept her gaze on Daniella's hands. "Not something I can pronounce."

That might have been true, but it really wasn't an answer. And Daniella realized she wasn't going to get one.

"What am I supposed to do to monitor it?" she asked.

"I'd like to see you daily," Dr. Sylvenia said. "We'll go inside one of these rooms and see what the sensors pick up."

She took a deep breath and raised her head.

"So," she said. "Tell me one more thing and then we're done. How's your back?"

Daniella focused on it, but didn't feel the pain she had felt earlier in the day—or in the trip—or whatever was going on.

"It feels fine," she said. "Whatever you did worked."

"Backs are tricky," Dr. Sylvenia said. "You'll let me know about the littlest twinge."

That wasn't a request. It was a command.

"I will," Daniella said.

"All right," Dr. Sylvenia said. "Then we're done. You're cleared to go to your room."

Daniella frowned. "That's all well and good, but I have no idea where my room is."

"Your data dot has the information," Dr. Sylvenia said. "You'll be able to access it when you leave the medical area."

Then she stopped reciting orders as if she was following a script. Her expression softened.

"Take care of yourself. You're going to need rest. You've been through a lot."

"So have you," Daniella said.

To her surprise, Dr. Sylvenia teared up. Then she rubbed her fingers under her eyes.

"Yeah," she said after a minute. "Yeah. We all have."

And left it at that.

———— ••• ————

DANIELLA SOON DISCOVERED that finding her room wasn't as easy as it sounded. She had the room number and access to a map, courtesy of a bunch of those opaque screens floating around, but that didn't make the journey any clearer.

She had to go through wings and floors and use the occasion elevator to reach the top passenger level, which was what she booked oh, so long ago. She had figured she needed a splurge.

Back then, she had had no idea just how much she would need that splurge.

She finally found the door, the only one in a slight cubby in what until now had been a smooth wall. The sharp angles of the little cubby made her realize everything on this floor curved ever so slightly. The sharpness of the little built-in walls near her door looked out of place.

The door unlocked as she neared it, which was a feature she would disable once she got inside. It seemed so convenient, and it wasn't safe. What if someone had come with her? What if she didn't want that someone in her room? That someone could just reach forward and yank the door open, and push her inside.

Her heartrate went up at the thought, and she shook her head at herself. Until this week, she had thought her stalker was the worst thing that had ever happened to her.

She put her hand on the door and let herself inside.

The room she entered was huge. It curved along the outside of the ship. The window coverings were up, revealing a starscape that looked unfamiliar to her.

She couldn't tell if the ship was moving or not, and she didn't care.

She pushed the door closed and stepped inside, wrenching her gaze from those windows. On the forms she had to fill out when she booked this place, she had asked for traditional furniture in the style of Europe and the west on Old Earth.

That meant chairs and tables, beds that were raised up from the floor, and counters in the kitchen. The instructions for everything, which floated beside her, probably downloaded through her data dot, were in the correct language, and the color scheme was soft blues and grays, avoiding bright reds and oranges as she had insisted.

The interior soothed her the moment she closed the door and, she suspected, that wasn't just because of the design. It was also because there was the soft scent of vanilla everywhere, a smell that she found calming.

So the high price she was paying for this stateroom was worthwhile, although not for the reasons she had initially booked it.

She was a tiny bit embarrassed about the size. With all the extra passengers, this room could have been split between several of them. Or an entire family could have been here.

But she wasn't going to offer it up, at least not yet. First, she had to take care of herself.

Usually when she traveled, she would get to her lodgings and walk through them to make sure everything was to her liking. But she didn't have the energy to visit the single bedroom with the private bath off to the side. Not yet, anyway.

She saw one of her favorite sweaters draped over a chair inside that room, though, which meant that her luggage had gotten here.

That was a relief. The fact that she was here was also a relief. She hadn't realized just how stressed she was not to have a place where she could be by herself. She needed time to review what had happened, how she felt, and what she had learned.

Someone had left fresh fruit on the countertop. Small bananas, mangos and bits of pineapple, along with oranges, apples, and dates. There was bread in its own little clear box, a loaf that looked like rye, another that looked like sourdough, and still another that was neither, with seeds and something that looked like it might be raisins scattered along the top. In another clear box, she saw pita, and in a third, there were crackers and chips of various hues. Clear jars filled with sauces lined the back wall, all of them labeled.

Each table—and there were several, from end tables to a dining table—had little bowls of mixed nuts on them.

The food lured her. She went into the half kitchen and lifted the clear lid on the bread. As she looked closer, she realized all of the bread had been sliced, so she took one piece of rye and set the lid back down. Then she opened a jar labeled cheese spread, and used it as intended, then sprinkled the top with dates. She hadn't grabbed a plate before she had done this, but she found one near her hand when she finished, which, she had to admit, made her feel ever so slightly creepy.

But she had signed waivers (those damn waivers again) that stated that she would be monitored in all places on the ship except her sleeping quarters and the bathrooms. Apparently that meant the living room of staterooms as well.

She placed her snack on the plate and carried it to the table near the curved windows. As she sat down, her back relaxed. Suddenly, she was shaking. She was having a reaction; she knew that much. She also knew that eating would help.

So she made herself eat as she stared at the stars.

She had never imagined this. For the first time in her life, she felt lost. She had gone from her parents' home to the college of their choice. There had never been any doubt she would go there.

And sure, she had picked a major that no one expected after a class had inspired her.

She liked thinking on a vast, global scale. Sometimes on a solar system spanning scale. She liked translating that kind of thinking into cities, and so her designs had become very popular.

She was good at thinking big. But thinking about things on a minute scale—such as why there had been toxic materials on that bridge—discombobulated her. She couldn't wrap her mind around any of it, nor could she think clearly about what had happened to her.

She closed her eyes for just a moment . . .

———— ••• ————————

. . . and woke up, hours later, her head tilted to one side, her neck pulled and aching. Her elbow was trapped between the arm of the chair and her body, threatening to cut off circulation throughout.

But her mind was clear, maybe for the first time since she got here. She had an image in her head of the explosions—not as they happened to her (she only remembered the one) but as they were described.

She remembered the partial map she had studied before coming to Tiberious—Grandea, on the edge of a mountainous region in one of the few habitable zones, and then the headquarters of Enjoyable Cruises, in that extra-large building on the top of the mountain, far enough away that she had questioned why they weren't in the city.

Then there was the mountain itself, with its fake cloud cover, the other peak hidden from view deliberately, the boarding bridges to space yachts, and the hasty rescue of everyone who needed to go.

She didn't believe that Dr. Sylvenia was noble—no offense to Dr. Sylvenia—but upending your entire life to be with a few patients in a moment of crisis was not the usual behavior of a doctor who was working for a corporation like Enjoyable Cruises.

Something about Sylvenia's expression told Daniella that Sylvenia believed that the space station might be a target as well, especially since two of the ships had blown up, presumably on the docking ring nearby.

Daniella sat up straight and shook out her arm, rubbing the elbow. There was a dent in her skin where the armrest had poked her. She made herself stand up, half expecting to be dizzy, but she wasn't.

Instead, she went into the bedroom to make sure all of her things had arrived.

The bedroom was slightly cooler than the main room. The shades were drawn on the windows, as if someone from outside could see in—even though she knew that wasn't true. Everything on the window-side of her stateroom was on the outside wall of the ship—or at least, what passed for an outside wall.

She had been told by a ship designer once that humans expected to have windows to the outside wherever they went, but that wasn't practical in most large ships. The ship needed to protect its interior. So either the ship had windows that looked onto a projection or there were several layers of material between the windows and the actual outside.

There was a large bed pushed up against the far wall on a beautifully carved bedframe. The headboard looked like it had been made of some kind of ebony, even though that too was probably an illusion. Black and white pillows in geometric shapes were piled against it, with the same pattern on the spread itself.

It did not look inviting so much as staged, which helped her. She wanted to find her own possessions and the only thing she saw was that sweater, folded over the back of a chair near an end table.

But her clothes were hung up in a surprisingly large closet, her luggage tucked beneath. The case she had marked *Do not open* did not look like it had been touched at all, except to be moved.

It was that case she grabbed now, finding her own personal devices, many of which carried her research as well as her entire work history.

Since she had been seriously thinking of that career change, she had come prepared.

Her neck still ached. She ran a hand over the sore muscle, wishing it would ease, then lifted the case upwards and placed it on her knees. She had her own network access point, although she knew it wouldn't work if the ship was actually traveling.

But the admitted illusions made her wary.

She wasn't going to access any shipboard systems until she checked all of this with her own systems.

She straightened out her legs, making sure they were between the floor and her devices. She didn't want her devices to touch anything inside the room, just in case the system here automatically logged her in.

If the ship's authorities were to be believed—and she wasn't sure about that—then they weren't going to invade her privacy in this room. So it was the only one that gave her even a chance of private communications.

Her system came on with no problems, but she couldn't ping Grandea like she had done before she left for the Enjoyable Cruises Headquarters. Nor could she access her personal communications system, the one that would privately attach her to everyone at her job.

So the ship probably was in transit, which made sense, considering how terrified everyone was of another attack.

But, that meant that all of the information she was going to get about what happened would be filtered through the ship itself.

Before she subjected herself to that, she opened her

research files, and did the in-depth investigation she had planned to do before she left.

She had downloaded a lot of files—current and historical—about Tiberious, Grandea, and Enjoyable Cruises. But she hadn't gone through most of them. A work project had gotten in the way.

Now, she investigated the sector, and discovered that it had been here longer than any place her company, the Urban Dwelling Initiative, had worked in the past fifty years.

That confirmed her sense of Grandea: she had thought when she arrived that everything looked like it had been baked into the soil of the place. The arrivals port had been old enough to be missing two major technological updates, and it would have made her nervous if she hadn't done any research at all.

She had only done the minimum before she booked.

She had learned that Enjoyable Cruises had its own tech and its own port, which was considerably newer because the company was newer. The ships were also supposed to be state of the art, and if the parts she had already seen, including this stateroom, were any indication, it was.

She had to straighten her back just a little, and move her head around before diving deep into the research.

Some of the discomfort she felt now was the kind she felt when she was creating an initial city plan. She had risen far enough in the ranks to design two kinds of city plans. The first was for new cities that were going to be built on previously unsettled lands.

That plan required her to look at a variety of factors, from the on-the-ground location to the resources nearby to the history of the entire region. And then she had to examine what other cities (if any) existed in the region, in the hemisphere, on the planet. And finally, she had to look to see what was in orbit, where the landing ports were for ships, and whether or not there were space ports in that region of space.

Sometimes she had to take into account satellites and moons; sometimes she had to factor in the politics of that entire slice of space. She needed to know if the city was going to be part of a major government or was going to be its own city-state. She had to know if it needed protection —from land, from any kind of sea, from the skies and of course, from orbit.

New cities were always the most work and the most fun. But the older cities were the most challenging. Because she could never do a complete redesign. She usually had to handle a new neighborhood or a new urban center.

A few times, she had to move a city because the first time it had been built, it had been built on dangerous terrain, which the original founders had not known about.

Sometimes in moving those cities or rebuilding them for the new political era, she realized how vulnerable they were to attack, how their previous existence was going to influence what they would become.

It intrigued her that the explosions had happened at headquarters and had had an impact on the boarding bridges, but the tumble-entry had been fine. Or at least, had been fine when she was there.

The space yachts had worked well enough to get her and many of these passengers to the *Starlight Skyline*.

Then there was the *Starlight Skyline* itself. Of the three ships, it had been slated to leave last, which meant that if the others were blown up on the space dock, the *Starlight Skyline* should have blown up there too.

The other ships were destroyed—or at least, that was what the initial meeting had implied. But it had also implied that they were damaged with the destruction of the boarding bridges, which was not possible, given what Dr. Sylvenia said. Those bridges took passengers to space yachts, not to the ships.

Yet all of the passengers from all three ships had been moved to the *Starlight Skyline*. Either she hadn't been docked when the explosions happened, implying that she had been in transit from somewhere else, or the other ships were collateral damage, just like the headquarters might have been.

Collateral damage or a distraction.

Because if Enjoyable Cruises was the target, then whomever caused the explosions should have taken out the headquarters, the space yachts, and the space dock.

Something should have happened at that space port, and maybe the mountaintop that held the tumble-entry should have been destroyed too.

But there had been enough time to get Daniella out, and to get others out. Her luggage had made it to this ship, which meant a lot of things had functioned correctly. And there had been an awful lot of people in that auditorium, including a lot of seriously injured folks.

The Enjoyable Cruises staff might have thought that they were the ones under assault, but that might simply have been a normal human bias. The loss of the headquarters and two ships allowed them to believe that—might have even made them believe it—but that might not have been intentional.

And her training always took her to look at other factors, factors most people did not consider, which was why her city plans were among the most in-demand in the sector.

She needed to research the region, just like she would if she had been assigned mapping for a new urban center. She had some of the information she needed; she would have to pull the rest from the system provided by the cruise line itself.

That last bit made her wary. She didn't know what they would think about her researching the area they had just left. Maybe they would consider it curiosity, since she had been through an ordeal, or maybe they wouldn't be monitoring her right now.

After all, they had a lot to deal with, and according to her doctor, Daniella was nearly done with the treatments she needed from them.

Her back was still a bit wobbly, though, so she grabbed almost a dozen pillows off the bed and made a little nest for herself. She put two pillows between her back and the bed frame, and she put her devices on top of pillows as well.

Then she opened her devices again, making sure she wasn't on any network but her own, and went to work.

As usual, she lost herself in the research.

Some of the questions she couldn't find answers to were about what happened. The *Starlight Skyline* had left before news filtered in about the surrounding areas—or perhaps the news had been blocked.

What she did know was this: when the ship left space dock, the space station was still intact. The dock had been compromised because the *Celestial Dreamer* and *The Moonlit Mirage* had exploded while docked. They had been on opposite sides of the dock. The *Starlight Skyline* was on a third part of the dock.

The three ships had formed a triangle, which was standard procedure. The part of the ring with the *Skyline* had detached as the other explosions happened—again, a preventative measure because ships often had issues in space dock, and they had to be dealt with on their own.

She doubted any builder had planned for two ships of that size to be mostly destroyed simultaneously. But the builder should have known that having more than one ship explode in space dock was possible. In fact, if she had been designing the space dock, she would have planned for a full-fledged attack that went after all of the ships.

That was the thing she kept tripping on. Nothing really made sense. If someone was going to do their best to destroy Enjoyable Cruises, then why didn't they destroy the *Starlight Skyline?*

The headquarters, the bridges, the ships. They all should have been destroyed all at once, along with the parts of the space station that were affiliated with Enjoyable Cruises.

But there was a definable path that had gone from the destruction to the *Starlight Skyliner*. People had been moved to the only remaining ship, which implied that a lot of time had passed before she had gotten here.

Which meant that no matter how terrified everyone was, they had gotten this ship up and moving.

What she had heard in that auditorium implied that the attacks happened all at once, and then stopped. So perhaps, the perpetrators had been caught.

Or something else happened. Something bigger.

Maybe something had happened in Grandea or to Grandea itself or to the transport system that brought most of the passengers to the headquarters.

Still, it felt very focused on Enjoyable Cruises, but that might have been because she had only received information about Enjoyable Cruises. She hadn't learned about any other company or any other part of the region.

Maybe she could find out that information. Maybe the wheels of gossip had finally started turning.

She would figure that out. She had an appointment the following day with the doctor. Maybe if Daniella went to lunch first, she might be able to overhear conversations, or create some on her own.

Right now, though, she needed rest. She clearly didn't have the energy she had had when she left on this trip.

She climbed over the pillows, sprawled on the gigantic bed, and fell sound asleep.

• • •

SHE WOKE up later than she expected, only giving herself a few hours before that appointment.

She showered, dressed in loose, comfortable clothes, and ate an apple, studying a ship's map as she did so.

The *Starlight Skyliner* was vast, bigger than some cities she had designed, bigger than most she had lived in.

No wonder the ship had room for all those extra passengers. If the map she was looking at could be believed, the ship could fit another ship's worth of passengers and maybe even one more.

This was the biggest ship in the line, and it was apparently used for a lot of things besides simple cruises. That meant there had to be some parts to the ship that the passengers here for a cruise would never see.

That pinged her suspicious brain as well.

As the brochures and vids showed, each little section of the ship was a neighborhood. The neighborhoods themselves were large enough that if she wanted to walk around the edges of one, it would take her hours. Not that most people did that more than once.

The neighborhood had everything a person could want from restaurants to concert halls (although not as big as that auditorium they had been in) to little shops to small hydroponic gardens that supposedly gave a sense of the outdoors.

The light here, on what the ship's map called the topmost level, mimicked Earth sunlight, which had long been deemed the healthiest form of light for human beings. Everything on the holo version of the map was bathed in light, and looked inviting.

It probably was.

What her engineering brain noticed the most, though, was that the passengers didn't have to mingle at all. In fact, it would be hard to get to another area—another neighborhood. Even the walking paths around the ship— and there were dozens—usually kept people at the edges of neighborhoods, where they could stop and look at the views outside the ship or watch a mobile map, showing them exactly where they were.

The neighborhood design also kept the staff isolated.

Her neighborhood had exclusive staff, as did all of the others.

Daniella had to dig into the map to find the actual overall staff, the people in charge of the ship proper, from the captain to the ship's engineers to the maintenance crews that worked on important systems, not the illusions that surrounded her.

The one thing she couldn't find was the specs. She couldn't find—even in the brochures she had kept— exactly how big this ship was and what its maximum capacity was.

It had been registered initially with a government that did not make ships follow those kinds of requirements, and then it was grandfathered into Enjoyable Cruise's fleet of ships.

It was the only ship like that in the entire fleet. Enjoyable Cruises had more than a dozen ships, and all of them except the *Starlight Skyline* were made and launched not too far from headquarters.

Three quarters of them were completing journeys elsewhere, and had been nowhere near the headquarters when this attack happened.

She had hoped she would be able to get to the main crew so that she could ask questions, but that quick look at the map—which had turned into a much longer look than she expected—had disabused her of that notion.

If she was going to talk with the main crew, she would have to make an appointment.

Just from the way the ship was structured, she wasn't even going to be able to bump into them in passing.

So she had to go with the gossip for the moment, and then see what was next. There was an information stand in the middle of her neighborhood, and she would go to that when she was good and ready. She expected a little information stand like that might have an automated system that would give her pre-programmed answers.

But these were extreme days and extreme circumstances, so the ship might have assigned a person there. Daniella was also paying enough that she might get personal service—or what seemed like personal service.

She let herself out of her stateroom into the long and empty corridor. The map had shown several side doors that would lead to any place she wanted to go in the neighborhood.

She wanted to be around people, so she ruled out the hydroponics, and stayed away from shops, at least for the moment.

She finally decided on a food bar. A large one flanked a water feature on her side of the neighborhood. She was a bit uncertain about visiting a water feature, but she wanted to see it. It might be a way to start a conversation with the other passengers.

The ship provided several routes around the neighborhood, most of them easy on the body. She was still exhausted from her ordeal, but she decided to walk anyway.

The walkway was designed the way that boarding bridge had been designed—curved walls and a curved ceiling along with a floor that had a carpet runner down the middle.

Only this floor had another carpet underneath, apparently part of this side of the ship's constant quest for maximum comfort.

She wasn't sure she liked the similarity to the processional, but at least she was alone. And the curved walls didn't open onto the outside; they showed views from inside the ship.

She had no idea if those views were a live feed or if they had been curated to show passengers enjoying themselves at various activities. Her engineering brain said it would be easier to have curated programming, but her heart wanted to see people having a good time.

She went down some stairs—if stairs was what they could be called. There was a step, and then a long landing, and then another step, and then another landing. This entrance was designed for another processional, with room on each landing for a number of people to pose.

There were no people today. She was alone. And she remained alone as she finished all ten of those steps, and headed into the food bar.

It was a see-and-be-seen place, with lots of tables right up front. The bar itself, where the various dishes were displayed, was in the center of the exceedingly large room. Aisles went down the middle and the sides, again past a lot of tables, so that whoever wanted to could greet people or pose with them or be near them or impress them or whatever it was they were supposed to do.

Every fifteenth table had someone in it. Often that someone was sitting alone, food half eaten, looking sad. If they caught her looking at them, they would avert their gaze. She didn't hear any conversation at all, even when people were sitting with each other. They focused on the plates of food before them or on the decorations around them, on anything but the woman walking past them.

And that made her more uncomfortable than she wanted to be, partly because she knew—as an engineer—that this was a walkway designed for people to interact.

But, to be fair, she wasn't sure she wanted to interact with these people either. She was beginning to understand, just from the walk, that she was obsessed with figuring out what had happened.

She tried to shake off that thought as she reached the bar. Images of food, most of them sandwiches, from Banh Mi to simple cheese on French bread to something more elaborate like a stacked chicken sandwich with pretty much everything on it, displayed on the case directly in front of her.

Another case showed so many soups she couldn't catalogue them. They were labeled from Tom Yum to Chicken Noodle to some kind of dumpling ramen soup. They looked soothing and inviting.

She didn't even go to the cases that showed individual

items like rice or potatoes or a single slice of bread. Nor did she look at the desserts yet, although given how lovely everything else looked, she might.

She had nothing but time, after all.

And that gave her a realization. She hadn't asked anyone if the events of launch had extended the trip time. She wasn't even sure she would arrive in time for her conference.

She now had a reason to go to the information desk after she finished with the doctor.

She got a personal-sized loaf of French bread, some almond butter, and the dumpling soup because it looked interesting. A little flag rose, and floated to her, along with instructions to pick a table and her food would find her.

She turned around, thinking that maybe she should sit on an aisle so that she could see people go by.

But habits long engrained made her go deeper into the food bar, away from easy access from other people.

An obvious family group lined the wall in the back, spread out in front of an image of the ship herself. There were ten people, all of them with similar features, dark straight hair in various different cuts from a bowl-shaped one to a cut that left the sides of the head shaved to another that left hair piled on top of the head. No one had any gray, although it looked like there were at least three generations, judging by the wrinkles and the fashion.

A baby of maybe a year bounced on a twenty-some-thing woman's lap, and the bounce, which brought the baby's chubby legs and bare feet onto the woman's thigh, made the baby laugh every time.

That sound, so joyful, almost seemed out of place here.

Daniella hadn't realized just how silent the food bar was until that baby's giggle.

She smiled at one of the older women, who did not smile in return. The look the woman gave Daniella was almost a warning look as in *Don't get near us*.

So Daniella didn't. She moved even deeper into the food bar, taking a table near a side wall. The flag had followed her. It attached itself to the flag holder, which lit up with a table number and her order and told her everything would arrive within a few minutes, and asked her if she wanted anything to drink.

She hadn't even considered that. She moved to a chair that would place her back to the wall as she thought about her options.

Then hands gripped her shoulders so hard that she let out a small shriek of pain. She couldn't turn around because the hands held her so tightly, and a voice spoke in her ear.

"Daniella! We meet again! Who would have thought?"

Her heart sank. She recognized this voice. It belonged to Ellis Amberson.

Her stalker.

He wasn't supposed to be anywhere near her. Her data dot had all of the pertinent information about him. It even forced places like this ship to comply by refusing to let her —and him—book trips on the same transport.

Something had gone wrong. And she was alone with him in this part of the food bar.

She did know how to deal with him, though.

She had dealt with him too much in those horrible early years. She had barely survived him.

But she *had* survived him. She had to keep that in mind.

That would keep the sheer terror at bay. She had learned, in dealing with him, that fear crippled her.

She didn't dare get crippled. She needed to think clearly and not let the muzziness since the explosion return.

Her main priority? Getting safely away.

She would deal with the other implications of his appearance later.

To get away, she didn't dare challenge him or even pretend to be anything but pleased to see him.

The last thing she wanted to do was make him mad.

"Ellis," she said in the most reasonable tone she had. "I was injured getting on this ship. Your hands are aggravating that injury."

"Oh!" He lifted his hands off her shoulders. He sounded surprised. She recognized this pattern. This was charming Ellis, the one who wanted to woo her so that he could be in control of her later.

"I didn't realize you were one of the people hurt," he said.

His contrition, real or not, allowed her to step away from him. She turned around so that she could see him. She wasn't going to let him get near her if she could avoid it.

She moved ever so slightly so that the back of her chair was between them. She couldn't make herself smile at him, but she worked to keep her expression pleasant.

He looked very different than he used to. He was older and thinner, eyes sunken in what looked like a permanent sadness. His pointed chin seemed even sharper. His auburn hair had lost a lot of its luster.

When she had first met him in college, he had a hand-someness that always made people look at him sideways, no matter what their orientation. There had been some-thing about him that everyone wanted a part of.

That handsomeness had faded. Maybe if he actually smiled, his face might seem less rigid, but right now, it looked foreboding, the kind of face that would scare small children, like that little toddler several tables away.

"I'm sorry," he said in that fake sincere way of his. Once that fake sincerity would have roped her in. She would believe that he had understood that he had done something to hurt her, and he felt bad about it.

Now, though, she knew he didn't feel bad about anything that had to do with other people, unless that bad feeling was about the way they had treated him.

"I didn't mean to hurt you," he said, and it was all she could do to make some kind of snide comment, the kind that would make him very mad. "I hope the injury wasn't too bad."

"It was bad enough," she said, but didn't give him any details.

"That's awful," he said. "Imagine the odds of both of us being here. And then coming to this food bar thing at the same time. Who could have guessed it?"

She could have, if she had known he was here. He always found a way for both of them to be in the same place. That was why she had so many court orders against him.

They had been enforced until now. It helped (and she hated the word "helped" in this context) that he had nearly killed her the last time. Risk of harm led to every jurisdiction following the edicts of a different jurisdiction.

He couldn't be anywhere near her or he would be arrested.

Only on this ship, there was no one to arrest him.

She knew that he kept track of her, despite the court orders and the data dot preventative measures, and all of the exclusions and regulations. The idea of prison time didn't seem to bother him.

Maybe because the prison he had been sent to for the original crime—which ended up being merely battery instead of attempted murder—hadn't been that unpleasant.

She wrenched her thoughts back to the moment. One thing at a time.

"Aren't you pleased to see me?" he asked, his eyes twinkling. Even though she was doing her best not to be upset, he could tell that she was. And that made her mad.

She couldn't even do her breathing exercises to keep herself calm, because doing that would also let him know that she was upset.

"I . . ." God, she couldn't even think of a plausible lie. She had put him out of her mind, except in her preparations for the trip.

When she had booked her seat at the conference, she had told the organizers about him, and they had assured her that he wouldn't be able to get anywhere near it.

But, the main organizer had said in a vid conference called by her lawyers and theirs, *we can't guarantee that he won't be on the space station. We will notify them, and make sure he won't even see the conference. It'll be in its own bubble, so that no one who isn't supposed to be there can see it.*

She had thought that would be a risk, but she had considered it a risk worth taking.

"Aren't you going to ask me to sit down?" he asked.

"I'm sorry, no," she said, using that measured tone.

Just the simple *no* made his eyes narrow.

"This is my first time out of my room—" she carefully avoided the word *stateroom* "—and I really need to be by myself. I don't want to pass out right here, and the doctors said if I spent too much time in the company of others, that might happen."

Ellis narrowed his gaze, as if he was trying to figure out if she was lying.

"If you pass out," he said, "I'll get you help."

He sounded so sincere. That tone used to work with his old face. With the new one, settled into lines and wrinkles and thinness, the tone was at odds with his cunning expression.

"I'm sure you will," she said, "but I really don't want to pass out. So maybe we can make a pact to meet later and catch up."

He stared at her. The one thing she had learned over the years was that he always wanted her to be sincere. And if she could fake a sincere tone, she could convince him to stay away.

"You want to meet here?" he asked, and she wondered why he was stressing this place. Was there something malfunctioning in her data dot? Was that why he could track her here?

And how did he get on this ship with her on it? She was a registered passenger and had been for months.

He shouldn't have been able to get near it.

"That's a good idea," she said, careful not to let the sadness into her voice. She had liked the ambiance here, even though the place was nearly empty.

And she had wanted to try all the different foods. She had imagined herself sitting here, enjoying the trip, finally achieving the kind of relaxation that she had been promised.

Of course, it wasn't going to happen. Even if everyone calmed down after the attacks, she wouldn't be able to relax because now she would always be on edge, looking for him.

"Should we perhaps say dinner?" she said, trying to get rid of him before the food arrived.

"Dinner would be lovely." He grabbed a chair and pulled it back. "But so would staying and conversing now. I promise not to make you stressed."

His very presence stressed her.

"I really have to follow the doctor's orders," she said.

"But you wouldn't be following them at dinner either," he said, and then his eyes narrowed again. That narrowing always unnerved her. "Or were you planning not to show up?"

"I was planning to meet you." She could do the fake sincerity thing too.

"As usual, you're not thinking things through," he said, and sat down. "Good thing I'm here to help you."

The food arrived at that moment. A tray brought it, floating above the table for a second, as if uncertain where to land, considering there were two people here now, instead of the one that had ordered.

The tray finally settled the issue by lowering itself to the center of the table, becoming a part of it.

The food was beautifully laid out, the soup glistening in a deep white bowl, the small loaf alongside looking perfect and delicious. She could smell the garlic and the hint of lime, as well as the vegetable stock and the lemon grass.

Normally, the smells would have increased her hunger, but with Ellis here, the smells made her stomach turn. She couldn't imagine eating in front of him.

She couldn't imagine eating right now at all.

She let her knees wobble, and made herself seem even more unsteady than she was. She braced a hand on the top of the chair.

"I'm so sorry," she said. "I need to lie down. I'm not going to be able to eat. You're welcome to it."

"But I thought we could catch up." His voice had a slight whine to it.

"Yes, later, like we discussed." She didn't even have to work on making her voice thicker than usual. The nausea had worked its way into her throat.

"You said dinner, right?" he asked.

"Yes," she said. "I'm very dizzy." She stepped backwards. "I will let you know the exact time."

Then she inched away, knowing better than to run from him. Running from him would provoke him to run after her, and God knew what would happen after that.

She made it to the aisle before she turned her back on him. Even then, she didn't run. She walked as fast as she could, her heart pounding.

One of the couples, sitting at a table in the aisle, looked at her as if she was making them panic.

Maybe she was. Everyone was traumatized, after all.

The thought sent a shiver through her. Something pinged the back of her brain, but she couldn't think about it right now. Right now, she had to get out of here.

She reached the food bar, and then headed up the aisle she had originally walked along. The family was long gone and there seemed to be even fewer people in this area than there had been before.

She wove her way through a couple of tables, as if she was taking a shortcut. She wasn't. She just wanted to see if he was following her.

As far as she could tell, he wasn't. She couldn't see the table she had initially found, but no one was between her and the entrance to the food bar.

She scurried to the exit, thought about calling security right then and there, and decided against it.

She had to get away.

But she was happy that she had memorized the map. Because she knew how to get to the information booth, and near the information booth, she would be able to contact security.

One thing she did know: she wasn't going to go back to her room. Not if he could monitor her. If he had done something, put a tracker on her or altered her dot, she didn't want to lead him right to her.

It was hard not to run to the information desk. It was harder not to constantly look over her shoulder.

Now that she was away from him, the panic had set in. She had thought she was protected from him.

She had thought that, with the right precautions, she would be free of him for the rest of her life.

She had thought wrong.

———— ••• ————————

THE IRONIC THING was that she had never really had a relationship with him. Not like some people had with their stalkers.

She had met him in college, yes, but only because they had taken the same courses. Their interests and training collided.

He majored in engineering, just like she did. A therapist, assigned by the courts, had asked her if she believed that Ellis had majored in engineering because Daniella had.

And she didn't. He had been taking the courses long before she did. He was doing poorly in the upper-level Dynamics course. The college only allowed three tries to pass, and he was struggling with his second. The professor required all of the best students to work with the failing students on a project, just to see if the failing students could bring their grades up.

And that was what had brought Ellis to her. She had helped him. He finally understood kinematics, which had been dogging him from the start. He couldn't quite understand how to study motion without considering the force involved. She had little empathy for that: she figured that kinematics was easier to understand in its basic forms than a lot of the other things that the engineers were studying.

But she didn't lose patience. She found that teaching something she thought was easy made it even clearer in her mind. So she figured out how to talk, not just to Ellis, but to the other two students she had been assigned.

They discussed kinematics in relation to biometrics. Since two of the three (including Ellis) had had sports injuries and had to go through physical therapy, they understood biomechanical energy because they had experienced it firsthand.

Range of motion, he had said to her as if she had revealed the entire world to him. *It's so damn easy, and so damn hard.*

Later, when he had grabbed her outside her apartment, he had bent her arm back and snarled, *Range of motion. Yours is pretty damn limited.* And then he had bent her elbow back so far that she heard it snap before she felt it.

The pain was intense, but she hadn't screamed. Instead, she had said tearfully, *Why are you doing this? I helped you.*

And then you abandoned me, he said, shoving her

against the wall. Her body went through it part way, her head getting stuck in it, and he laughed.

Apparently, it was the sound of her going into that wall that alerted her neighbors, who called for help. Although no one had been brave enough to open a door. By the time the police arrived, Ellis had broken three of her ribs, punctured a lung, and slapped her until she was barely conscious. Ironically, it was only the wall that held her up.

He had been arrested, and tried, and evidence from his data dot showed he had been stalking her for the two years after that class they had together. The abandonment had been his interpretation of her transfer to a better university, where getting her undergraduate engineering degree would allow her to move forward with graduate studies in urban planning on a grand scale.

She had moved and hadn't thought of him for those two years, although looking back on it, she realized he had always been lurking. She would see him out of the corner of her eye.

After all of the medical procedures, after suffering through all of the legal proceedings, after feeling the humiliation of having her life examined by people who judged her rather than empathized, she learned that through it all, he had still monitored her every movement.

So instead of finalizing her degree, she spent what little money she had on hiring a service that would help her separate her life from his. Hence the suits that resulted in injunctions keeping him away from her. The mandates that led to the change in her data dot and his. Using the widespread information system to keep them apart—forever, she had thought.

Of course, she had to leave her preferred university and find another. She altered her coursework just a bit more, but that had turned out all right. There she learned how to combine all of her strengths—her engineering brain, her ability to see things on a vast scale, and her (relatively new) interest in keeping communities safe—into designing cities that worked, not just inside of themselves, but inside of regions, planets, and areas of space.

She had risen to the top of her field, and yes, she occasionally got reports about him, including how he had charmed the administration running the prison into thinking he of all people deserved early release.

But she had never thought it would affect her. She kept notifying any place she traveled to that he was not allowed near her, but that was just routine, bolstered by the free-flow of information, the protections in the data dots, and the agreements that each government had with the others.

She had thought she was safe.

It almost shattered her to think that she wasn't.

•••

BY THE TIME she reached the information desk, she had gotten angry. She wasn't going to be a woman who shattered. She was going to be someone who took action.

The information desk was in its own little kiosk, and to her surprise, a person stood behind it. Nearby signs that glowed as she stepped near it made her realize that the personal touch was something new, and it was probably designed for the higher end customers. Most people with money would rather have a human connection than an automated one. That way they felt like they got a personal experience, tailored to who they were.

She stepped inside the information kiosk with a bit of hope. The fact that this was enclosed meant that no one outside of the people in control would hear her request.

Still, she had learned long ago to be cautious. So she asked about the timeline first: would they arrive in time for her to attend her conference?

The woman behind the desk checked some partially visible screen, but it was clear her heart wasn't in it. She looked as tired and stressed as Daniella felt.

"We're doing what we can," the woman said. "It looks like you'll be a day or two early instead of four days early as you planned. I hope that works for you."

As if that would make a difference. Because if it didn't work for Daniella, there was nothing she could do about it.

"It does," she said, in her most reasonable voice. "Thank you."

She started to leave—which was performative—and then stopped and turned.

"I have one other issue," she said. "I need to speak to security. I need to do it privately and without anyone noticing that I was doing so. I can't go into any area marked security. Is there a way to do that?"

The woman looked up. The question seemed to revive her. "Is everything all right, ma'am?"

"No," Daniella said. "I have a very serious problem, one that is delicate and requires some finesse. Can you help me with that?"

"Certainly, ma'am," the woman said. "We have a waiting area. It is private, but it will cut off most recordings and tracking. Is that all right with you?"

All right? It was a blessing. But Daniella didn't say that.

"I would prefer as much privacy as possible," she said. "So, yes, that would be great."

The woman moved away from her desk, touched the glowing white wall behind her, and it opened into yet another room. That one looked utilitarian. It had only a few extra features which, Daniella knew, were the kind that couldn't be hacked.

"It may be a minute," the woman said.

Daniella didn't like the sound of that. If Ellis was tracking her, then he would be suspicious when he couldn't figure out where she was.

"I need someone as soon as possible," she said. "This is an emergency."

The woman looked at her disapprovingly. "Yet you had time to ask about your schedule?"

"I'm not going to discuss that with you," Daniella said. Her voice was starting to wobble. She cleared her throat to make it stop. She needed to sound firm. "I will discuss it with your security personnel."

"If it was an actual emergency," the woman said, her voice now matching her expression, "then you should have used the emergency—"

"I didn't dare," Daniella snapped. "I have a problem with a stalker, and I had to get away from him first. Now, I will wait in that little room, but if I'm there too long, he will find me, and that means he finds you, and that's not a good thing."

The woman's skin went gray. "I will get someone here immediately," she said.

Appealing to someone's self-interest always worked. Daniella hated the cynical feeling that accompanied the thought, but it was true.

The woman escorted her into the small room. It felt stuffy, and the lack of decoration made it seem even smaller. Daniella wanted to tell her not to close the door, but she also didn't want to be visible to anyone who came into the information kiosk.

So she watched warily as the door closed, and hoped to hell she wouldn't have to wait too long.

She didn't sit. Instead she paced. She was on her third time around the little rectangular space when a man slid inside.

She jumped. He was roughly the same size and build as Ellis. But this man was wearing a light brown uniform and he had a security tag on his shoulder. Another floated ahead of him, maybe to calm her or maybe to upset her, if she had been doing anything wrong.

"I'm Officer Montauk," he said, even though his identification and his credentials rose in front of her left eye. "I understand you have an emergency."

"I do," she said. "We might have to discuss this with someone in charge of the ship itself."

He gave her one of those *I'll be the judge of that* smiles, but to his credit, he didn't say that. Instead, he swept a hand at the chairs built into one of the walls.

"Would you like to sit?" he asked.

"No," she said. "I'm too tense to sit."

It was all she could do to keep from wrapping her arms around herself. She stopped pacing, but she still wanted to move. It took all of her control to keep herself from rocking back and forth.

She was nervous. Check that. She was scared to death.

"You've checked my files, right?" she asked.

"Yes," he said.

"You saw the injunctions, the court orders, the requirements to keep Ellis Amberson away from me?"

"Yes, of course," he said.

"Well, he's not supposed to be near me. He's not even supposed to be on this vessel. And he just ambushed me in the food bar on the ship's highest level."

Montauk's eyes glazed for a moment. He frowned.

"I see that you were talking with someone," he said. "A Mr. Elisand?"

"I don't know what name he's using, but check the dot, the DNA profile he had to give, and all the other identifying features." It was work to keep her voice level. She didn't want to yell at this man, and yet she would if she had to.

"All right," Montauk said, "just give me a moment."

He stepped back, and used a panel on a nearby wall, rather than his own data dot or whatever they needed to use inside of this little room.

He made a small *humph* noise, and then shook his head.

"You're right, ma'am," he said. "We will need to talk to someone higher up."

"If I go to your security room," she said, "there's a good chance he will track me. He's obsessed with me and has been for years. He's tracked as much as he could since he got out of prison, but the laws have successfully kept him away from me until now. And if you don't have the resources to safely protect me throughout this trip, I don't know what we're going to do."

"I understand, ma'am," Montauk said. "It's just that

this might require decisions that are not the kind I can make."

A chill ran through her. Something really was wrong, something bigger than Ellis's appearance.

"If you take me to security," she said, "and he knows it, it's going to enrage him. The last time he was around me and was enraged, he tried to kill me."

"I see that, ma'am." Montauk's voice was soft and soothing, but his eyes were narrow, and his expression a bit stressed. "We can move you through the corridors and give you protection."

"What does that mean?" she asked.

He reached into the pocket of his uniform and pulled out what looked like an external data dot. It was the size of her thumbnail and unmarked.

"This will block your location tracking. You will disappear from any service that allows someone to trace you."

She'd heard of things like that, but in Lakona and other places she had visited, they were illegal.

"Once we get you to the security level," he said, "you won't need it. The entire level is blocked off. No one can tell who is there and who is not."

Which made sense. She didn't like the idea of the external dot. The fact that Ellis had found her here made her wary. But she didn't see that she had any other choice.

She took the dot from Montauk, and clutched it between her thumb and forefinger. The dot was soft and squishy. It felt like she could crush it if she pushed too hard.

"All right. I'll trust it." Even though she didn't want to. "Let's go."

•••

THE WALK through the back corridors was an education in anti-design. Everything in the front-facing parts of the shop was lovely, brightly lit in the areas that needed a lot of Earth sunlight colors, sculptures attached to the walls made to catch the light and reflect it back or to absorb it near corners.

But back here, there was no design. It was all dark and gray, designed to push people from one part of the ship to the other as quickly as possible.

She and Montauk took corridors and elevators, and if she hadn't been paying close attention, she would have gotten confused and lost. The trip took her to the very center of the ship. He led her through a few more deliberately confusing corridors, even though the elevator they had taken to get there was part of a set of internal elevators that were scattered all over the back areas.

If they had stayed on one of the first elevators they had taken, and ridden it all the way to the center of the ship, they would have arrived at the exact same door much sooner than they did.

But she understood. Sometimes it was better that civilians did not know how to get from one part of a protected space to another.

Montauk opened the door into a room that was much wider than any of the corridors had been. The room was cooler too, with the same high arched ceilings that were in the passenger sections.

The light here was a calming pale blue, though, threaded with some Earth gold. There were work areas scattered throughout and team-building areas in the center, the kind she had been forced to design early in her career —forced because she hadn't believed that they worked (and later, studies had shown that they didn't work well at all).

There were more doors scattered around the walls, some with rotating blue colors, which she bet some kind of code. The officers here knew where each room led based on color; but there was no way she could know without having the key or having spent a lot of time here.

A woman walked over to her. The woman had a mass of braided black hair. Some of it was wrapped around the top of her head, and the rest flowed down her back.

Her features were angular, her eyes sharp.

"You're Daniella Obregón," she said. It wasn't a question, but Daniella answered it as if it was.

"Yes," she said.

"You will come with me," the woman said, and led her through one of those doors. This one was dark blue on top, but faded to a lighter blue on the bottom. It slid open sideways, letting her into a room where the darker blues predominated.

Daniella had a sense that if the woman desired it, the room could look as utilitarian and functional as the service corridors. Something about this room told her it was designed to have whatever impact on a person's mood that the woman wanted it to have.

"I'm Mirabel Lassiter, security chief on the *Starlight Skyliner*." She swept a hand toward a dark blue chair near a lighter blue table. Then she went to the other side of the table and put her hands on the sides of another chair, as if she was going to move it.

It was clear that she wanted Daniella to sit down, and this time, Daniella wasn't going to refuse.

She took her spot near the table, and sat with her back as straight as she could make it.

Lassiter remained standing, but she was hunching just a little, which made her seem more accessible.

"I am going to speak on behalf of the ship," she said. "We owe you an apology."

Daniella sat even straighter. No one in a position of authority had ever apologized to her before—not in her career, not in the judicial system, and certainly not that professor whose actions had brought her to Ellis's attention in the first place.

"There was a lot of confusion as we boarded the ship. We were able to move everyone from the *Moon-*

light Mirage and *The Galactic Dreamer*, but we had to do so quickly. Our system glitched, preventing everyone from boarding the *Starlight Skyline*, so we had to shut the system down to get the passengers on board."

Despite her best intentions to remain calm, Daniella felt a surge of adrenaline. That couldn't have been an accident. It had to have been deliberate.

Ellis had ended up with a degree in systems analysis and, one of her bosses had told her, he had followed that with systems design, courses he had taken in prison. He always applied for lower-level work on the same jobs that she headed.

Of course, she never saw those applications; they were denied simply because she was on the team.

"This is not an excuse." Lassiter moved to the front of the chair, sat down, and rested her elbows on her legs. The illusion of relaxation, the illusion of comfort, all designed to put Daniella at ease.

The apology might have been designed to put her at ease as well.

"But," Lassiter said, "there was a lot of confusion and quite a few moving parts. We believed the entire company was under attack and we had to leave quickly."

"Believed," Daniella said. "You've since discovered otherwise?"

Lassiter's eyebrows went up before she could catch herself. When she did, she forced her face into a rather sheepish smile. The look did not go all the way to her eyes, which were assessing Daniella.

Lassiter seemed surprised that Daniella caught the past tense.

"Yes, believ*ed*," Lassiter said, emphasizing the tense. "No other parts of the company were attacked after that day. Our space station offices remained fine. Our other locations throughout the sector were unharmed. None of our other ships were damaged as well. Some of our people believe that if this had been a system-wide attack, then everything would have been damaged."

Daniella nodded. She'd been dealing with the justice systems in various communities for years, sometimes because of her job, but early on because of the problems caused by Ellis.

She learned to be very careful when she spoke. She needed to be careful here. She didn't want to be blamed for something, but she also had to let Lassiter know what she was thinking.

"Before I got here," Daniella said, "you had a chance to look over my history, is that correct?"

"Yes," Lassiter said. She was sitting up a bit straighter now, as if she knew that something in the conversation had shifted. "That's why we're apologizing about Mr. Amberson's presence."

As you should, Daniella nearly said, but she didn't want to be confrontational. Not yet. She needed their help all the way on this long journey.

"I would hope you're going to do more than apologize," Daniella said.

Lassiter raised her chin. It was a small, subtle move, slightly defiant. She seemed braced for something difficult.

"He and I cannot cross paths again. You have to keep him away from me," Daniella said.

Lassiter relaxed just a bit. "We will be doing that. I should have said so from the start."

Yes, Daniella nearly said, *you should have.*

"What you need to understand," Daniella said, "is that Ellis has a lot of systems training. He can hack into a lot of older systems. I don't know what you're running here, but if you're only going to use your systems, then you have to realize that he might find me again." Daniella took a deep breath and straightened her back. "And you will find that I will not be understanding if that happens."

She didn't really want to issue a threat, but she felt there was no choice. Lassiter needed to know that Daniella would not be an easy passenger if she encountered Ellis again.

Provided, of course, she survived the encounter.

"We will protect you," Lassiter said. "We're already looking into our legal options. He found you. It took time, but he found you."

"It didn't take time," Daniella said. "It took less than two hours. I assume he couldn't get near my room, so he didn't try. But within two hours of me venturing out for the first time, he found me."

Lassiter's mouth thinned. The information was going in, but Daniella wasn't sure if Lassiter understood the import.

"He's clearly tracking me," Daniella said. "I assume he's using your systems to access my data dot."

She didn't add that she thought maybe he couldn't access anything near her room. She wasn't sure if that was true, so she didn't want to muddy up the conversation.

"I do know this, though," she said. "He will find me again, unless you figure out how to prevent it."

Lassiter frowned, then she looked away. Daniella couldn't tell if Lassiter was sharing this information or if she was simply trying to absorb what Daniella told her.

"He seems quite determined," Lassiter said.

Daniella suppressed a sigh. She hated talking to people in authority who only dealt with certain kinds of humans. People on cruise vessels had money, most of the time. The crimes here were probably crimes of passion, which were, by definition, unplanned. Or they were monetary crimes.

The crimes that came from the darker side of human nature, the ones planned by people who didn't care at all about others, usually didn't come into play in a vessel like this.

"Yes, he's determined," Daniella said, trying not to let her frustration show.

Maybe she did let some of it show, because Lassiter gave her another sharp look. "You said he's obsessed."

"Yes," Daniella said.

"Do you know why?" Lassiter asked.

And there it was: the stupid question every single person in authority asked when they didn't understand what Daniella was facing. She had learned over the years that getting angry didn't work. Nor did lengthy explanations.

People like Lassiter weren't trained in the range of human experience. They just rose through the ranks because they were good at making sure no one violated the rules on a cruise ship and because they could get someone who was impaired out of public view quickly.

"He's a stalker," Daniella said, keeping her voice level. "They're obsessives. There is no why. He will sacrifice everything—maybe even his life—to come after me."

Lassiter grunted, the kind of sound someone made when they learned a bit of information they might or might not believe.

Daniella braced herself for what was coming next.

"Forgive me," Lassiter said, and the tone was more than enough to tell Daniella the ancient questioning routine would start if Daniella didn't shut it down.

But she had to wait for the question first.

"I guess I'm not understanding," Lassiter said. "You're not a celebrity. You're not outrageously wealthy. So why you?"

The question wasn't quite what Daniella had expected. Men usually asked *What's so special about you?* as if they thought it impossible that someone would be obsessed with her. Those men were usually focused on her lack of beauty.

Lassiter was clearly used to a different class of people. Wealth, celebrity—those things meant that Daniella would be a candidate for obsession. But she was stunningly ordinary, on the outside anyway.

She wasn't ordinary; her engineering brain—her urban planning brain—was in demand all over the system. Therapists and a handful of knowledgeable law enforcement believed that Ellis was attracted to the way she thought and maybe even believed, in the early days, that he and Daniella would make a good team, if she only would be willing to work with him.

It was as good an explanation as any, but it was probably as wrong as Lassiter's assumption that only celebrities and the very rich were worth someone's time.

"I don't know why he's obsessed with me," Daniella said. "And you know what? It's not my job to know. It's *your* job to keep him away from me. You have all of the pertinent information. You know he nearly killed me once. You know that he shows up uninvited wherever he can. You know that his data dot is supposed to be set up so that he can't even be in the same city as me. And yet you people let him onto this ship."

Oh, she had devolved into a *you people*. She wasn't as calm as she thought she was.

Lassiter's expression had flattened, as if she wasn't used to someone talking with her like that.

Screw her. It was going to get worse if Daniella got injured (again) because of their inability to keep him off this ship. She would sue this company into oblivion if that happened. Although, truth be told, it looked like the company might be headed there anyway.

"How or why he's after me isn't important right now," Daniella said. "What matters is that you have to believe he will go to great lengths to get to me. He almost succeeded today. I managed to startle him when I let him know that I had been injured . . ."

She paused, as a thought rose in her brain. He hadn't known she was injured. More than that, he hadn't expected it.

She had studied Ellis over the years as well. The fact that he hadn't expected it meant that he had anticipated something about her—about seeing her here—and maybe he had anticipated it for a long time.

But there should have been no way to have anticipated this for a long time. The passengers shouldn't have been able to predict that two of the three ships departing at the same time would be destroyed, leaving the larger third ship to take the remaining passengers away.

They shouldn't have been able to predict that all of the passengers would be on the same ship, and that the systems would have to be shut down to let everyone board.

The systems . . .

Ellis knew about systems. Ellis would do anything to get to Daniella.

But even she was having trouble believing that he would go to such lengths to get close to her.

She couldn't finish the previous thought. She couldn't even remember the previous thought. Her mind had veered into a different direction.

Lassiter watched her, but remained silent. Normally, that would have bothered Daniella, but it didn't.

Her hyperfocus returned. Her brain was finally working.

"Did something happen in Grandea too?" she asked.

"What?" Lassiter asked. "Why?"

"Just tell me," Daniella said, as if this were her office instead of Lassiter's.

Lassiter tilted her head a little, as if she wasn't sure she should indulge Daniella at all.

But then Lassiter squared her shoulders and said, "We left the region quickly, but so far, the news we have gotten did not mention that Grandea was attacked or anywhere else on Tiberious was destroyed."

"And you would have heard, right? I mean, that's the largest city on Tiberious. Its destruction should have been news."

"I can't say for certain," Lassiter said, "but I would

assume we would have heard by now if Grandea was attacked. It seems clearer and clearer to us, at least, that this attack was focused on Enjoyable Cruises."

But Daniella didn't believe that either. Not anymore.

"Because your headquarters was attacked," Daniella said. "And the two ships."

"Yes," Lassiter said.

"But not the offices in the space station," Daniella said.

"That's right," Lassiter said.

"And not this ship," Daniella said.

"That's correct as well," Lassiter said.

"Even though this ship was at the same space dock as the other two ships," Daniella said.

Lassiter's frown grew deeper. "What are you getting at?"

It seemed impossible. It seemed too big. It seemed like something terrorists would do, not a single determined man.

"Do you know what motivated this attack?" Daniella asked. "Was there warning? A threat maybe—you know, if Enjoyable Cruises stayed away from some region or something. Was there anything like that?"

Lassiter shook her head as Daniella spoke. "Not to my knowledge. But that is not something I would be privy to."

"Really?" Daniella asked. "Because this ship goes all

over the sector. Wouldn't security need to know that some group was targeting the parent company?"

Lassiter let out a small breath. She stood up and walked to the main door, hands clasped behind her back. She clearly had to think about what Daniella had said.

Then Lassiter nodded. "Yes, of course they would tell me. And they had not said anything." She turned, her gaze on Daniella, as if trying to see through her. "So, to my knowledge, we have not had threats."

"Yet you all believe this was an attack on Enjoyable Cruises," Daniella said.

"What other interpretation do we have?" Lassiter asked.

Daniella leaned back in her chair. She hated the directions her brain was going in right now, but that was what people hired her for. They hired her for her different perspectives on the universe around them, her different ways of putting pieces together.

Although, right now, she was worried that she was being too internal, too self-involved.

Still, it was the only path she had to explore.

"Tell me," she said. "Is it in your handbook to shut off the scanning protocols for data dots in an emergency?"

Lassiter drew herself to her full height. Her cheeks flushed. "We don't have that sort of protocol. We're a safe vessel for travel. We do—"

"Please," Daniella said. "You were in a hurry to save

our lives—which is as it should be—and because you were, you moved passengers from one ship to another. The system shut down, so you didn't wait for it to boot back up."

Lassiter crossed her arms. "That's right. It's procedure. If a ship is in distress, for example, we move its passengers to the nearest ship."

"Once the system came back up, though," Daniella said, "did you scan the passengers? Run the material on their data dots again?"

"Why would we?" There was an edge in Lassiter's voice. "They had already been admitted to one of our ships. All of the passengers have been cleared."

"Yes," Daniella said, "except for conflicts like mine. Do you scan for that?"

"Of course. When you book." Lassiter did sound offended now. "We're quite rigorous about that."

"I'm sure you are," Daniella said, keeping her voice level. She didn't want to offend Lassiter even more. "But, when you move passengers from one ship to another in a crisis, do you rescan?"

"No." Lassiter closed her mouth tightly. "No, we do not. But what would you have us do? Have passengers choose lots? We have to leave this passenger behind because they're not supposed to be on the same ship as that passenger?"

Daniella actually felt calm in the face of the anger. She felt like she had an answer now.

"It's a hole in your system," she said. "It's—"

"We can't prevent people from boarding an emergency ship!" Lassiter said, her voice wobbling. The stress of the last week was clearly showing with her too. Daniella doubted that Lassiter had done anything to take care of herself since this entire crisis began.

"Of course you can't," Daniella said. "Nor should you."

"Then what is this about?" As if Lassiter didn't know. And maybe she didn't.

Daniella was going to take this slow, because she wasn't certain. "First," she said, "you'll need to fix the system."

"We can't leave—"

"Hear me out," Daniella said. "When you bring on emergency passengers, you rescan them for conflicts. If there are any, then someone—and that'll be up to you, maybe based on how much they've paid—will have to be restricted to certain parts of the ship."

Lassiter's mouth pinched, but then she nodded. The idea clearly made sense to her.

"I will put that into the company as our new protocol," she said. "I'm not sure when, however, because we have this emergency to deal with."

As if Daniella had forgotten it.

"Which is my other point," she said. "This may have been a set-up to get someone onboard this ship—"

"As in Mr. Amberson?" Lassiter's voice was filled

with sarcasm. "Really, do you think he'd go to those kinds of lengths to get to you?"

"I would hope not," Daniella said. "But he might be our window into what really happened."

Whatever reaction Lassiter had expected from Daniella, that wasn't it. And the logic of it seemed to calm Lassiter down.

"What do you mean?" Lassiter asked.

"I'm sure your system has a hierarchy of rules about who can and cannot board, am I right?"

Lassiter looked at her sideways. "Yes."

"And it might depend on who else is traveling, just like me, or it might be because of cargo—as in you might be carrying something exclusive and expensive for someone—am I right?"

"Yes." Lassiter's response was firmer this time.

"And it might also depend on the stops along the way. A passenger might have been banned from a community that the *Starlight Skyliner* might dock in briefly, so that passenger would have to take the *Moonlight Mirage,* which won't stop at that community, even though both ships were going to end up at the same destination. Right?"

Lassiter cursed. Then she put her hand to her forehead, and cursed again.

She hadn't thought of the possibility of a passenger using an emergency to access an area they had been banned from. Since she hadn't thought of it, that meant no one had, or she would have had procedures for it. It was a problem. People loved to find holes in systems. That was why Daniella was so cautious when she designed her cities. She made sure there were as few holes as possible.

"And then there is that tiny moment when the protocols are off," Daniella said. "A good systems expert might be able to slide into your entire system and view passengers' personal information, as well as their financial information. Someone might not access the financial information here, but that might not stop them from doing it later."

Lassiter frowned. If nothing else, she would argue for the protocol change quickly. Maybe even as this ship traveled to its first stop.

But Daniella wasn't done. She couldn't help herself. She got this kind of focused on the job, and that focus had transferred here.

So she asked, "How many times in the past year have there been emergencies with Enjoyable Cruise's ships?"

Lassiter let her hand drop. "Not that many. But more than in the previous few years."

"Someone figured out your system," Daniella said. "They've been testing it, maybe even using it."

Lassiter shook her head, almost as if she couldn't believe it. She sighed.

"I will inform the investigators as soon as possible," Lassiter said. She seemed to be thinking out loud. "That way they can see if there's any indication that your theory is correct."

Daniella's stomach clenched. As usual, her brain was ahead of the conversation, and had already come up with a solution.

She wasn't sure she liked it.

"We can find out if the theory is correct," Daniella said.

"There is no 'we,'" Lassiter said, shaking her head. "You have done more than enough. I can't let you into our systems to figure out what has gone wrong."

Daniella smiled despite how she was feeling. "I would never suggest that," she said. "We just have an opportunity here—well, you do. I do not think it was a coincidence that Ellis was here to take advantage of the hole in your protocols."

Lassiter made that tight little disproving expression. "I cannot believe that one man would—"

"I don't think so either," Daniella said. "But hear me out. As I said, Ellis Amberson has a lot of systems training. He has also spent time in prison. It would not surprise me if he learned to sell his systems expertise to criminals to help them beat the protocols most businesses have set up to block people from their premises or to prevent people from traveling across borders that they shouldn't be crossing."

Lassiter stared at her. "You believe Mr. Amberson would damage ships and kill people to get to you?"

That was a good question. Years ago, Daniella would have said no. But she didn't know the sharp-faced Ellis who had confronted her a few hours ago, the man who clearly had no charm at all, the man who probably couldn't convince anyone of anything.

"The man I knew was a loner," Daniella said. "But remember, he tracks me. And if he knew there was going to be an attack on Enjoyable Cruises, and he saw that I was going to be on one of the ships, I believe he might have taken advantage of that."

Lassiter had crossed her arms again.

"I have learned the hard way," Daniella said, "that there are no coincidences when it comes to Ellis and his obsession with me."

It took work to keep her voice from shaking. But she needed to face this, because she needed information. She couldn't live with the idea that his appearance had been a coincidence.

"All right," Lassiter said. "You see an opportunity. What is it?"

Daniella took a deep breath. She knew if she made this proposition, she would not be able to take it back.

But she felt like she had to do it, if for no other reason than those people who had been so happily walking ahead of her on that processional, and a few minutes later were lying dead on the floor of the boarding bridge.

"What I'm going to propose," Daniella said, "is risky.

I will need your guarantee that your people will protect me."

"My people will always protect you," Lassiter said.

"Except when they fail, like this afternoon," Daniella snapped.

Lassiter grimaced. "Point taken. But from now on, we will do everything in our power to make sure that you are safe."

"Good," Daniella said, "because here's what I think we should do."

— ••• —

THE PROPOSAL WAS SIMPLE ENOUGH: she would get Ellis to confess. She was confident that he would if she pushed him correctly. The problem was that she had two ways of pushing him. One would make him brag; the other would make him furious.

The problem was that she wasn't sure which method would work.

And, she wasn't quite sure what this version of Ellis would do when he was angry.

She hadn't told Lassiter any of those things, and it had still been hard for Lassiter to go along with the plan. She didn't want a civilian to involve herself in the ship's business. She didn't like the fact that the entire meeting would be outside of her control.

And she worried about liability. A lot. She kept coming back to it, over and over again, saying that the ship would be liable if anything happened to Daniella.

Finally, to force Lassiter to stop making the argument, Daniella had said in her most reasonable voice, "You realize you're already liable for everything that happened to me here? I'm sure one more liability issue won't really matter."

That shut Lassiter up, and finally got her to agree to the plan.

Which was good, because Daniella wanted to execute the plan immediately. She was afraid that if she slept on it, she would change her mind by the time she woke up in the morning.

She needed Ellis to find her. She almost went back to the food bar, but she really did want to sample all of its wares during the rest of the trip. If this worked, she would be able to do that.

She held that out to herself as a reward for a job well done. A successful execution of a plan that terrified her to her very core.

So, she ruled out the food bar, and let Lassiter pick a different location. Lassiter even offered to enhance Daniella's presence on the network, so that Ellis would notice where she was, and scurry over to join her.

Lassiter picked a fancy appetizer restaurant that was ten times more expensive than the food bar—not that it mattered to Daniella.

But it might matter to Ellis.

She had no idea how he was doing financially. For all she knew, if he had hacked into the system to find her, he could hack into the system to handle his own finances as well.

So she tried not to worry about where she was. She had realized, though, that she worried about everything when it came to Ellis. When she tried not to worry about what he would do to her, she worried about something adjacent.

That was an old coping mechanism, one she thought she had abandoned. But she was voluntarily re-entering the fray with him, and so it shouldn't have surprised her that the old coping mechanisms had returned.

Before leaving Lassiter, Daniella used the security system to cancel her doctor's appointment. She didn't want Ellis to be waiting for her near Dr. Sylvenia's office.

After leaving Lassiter, Daniella went immediately to the restaurant. Like most places on the ship right now, the restaurant was mostly empty and the best tables were available.

She chose a round white one near the enhanced water feature. It had enough real water that occasionally a droplet would hit her face or her hand. Most of the water flowing up and over the sculpted center, though, was an optical illusion, just like she had suspected.

The water in the basin of the sculpture was a deep blue, one that only occurred in the deepest part of oceans when they were hit with the right kind of light. So she took that to mean that most of the water in the sculpture was an illusion.

Still, she missed the slight sound that real fountains made, the hint of rain on a lake. Sometimes illusions just didn't work.

But that didn't stop the area from being pleasant. It was illuminated by rays of light that resembled slanted rays from Earth's sun, finding their way through trees to a forest floor.

There were no trees here, and the floor was a matching yellow gold that reflected those rays, but the entire scene warmed her at a time when she really needed the warmth.

She ordered some cornflower soup from the floating menu, but used the menu option that would allow the soup to arrive fifteen minutes after she ordered it. The thing she wanted—the thing Lassiter suggested she get first—was a yellowish gold mixed drink, the specialty of the house, a non-alcoholic mixture of liquids Daniella hadn't heard of, but which tasted of lemon grass mixed with sugar, and was enhanced with something fizzy.

It tickled Daniella's nose, and would have pleased her if it weren't for her nerves. She initially thought she was just going to stare at the water feature, but she couldn't stop herself from looking around.

She told herself that was okay; Ellis would recognize the moves. She used to do that same kind of searching look when he had been after her the first time. She had always suspected that in those days, he would stand just out of her range of vision and watch her long before he came over.

He would probably do that here as well, even though she didn't want him to. She wanted to get this over with.

She crossed her legs, and swung the top leg as if she didn't have a care in the world. Or maybe the gesture just made her look as nervous as she actually was; she had no idea which.

And it probably didn't matter.

The one thing she was afraid of the most, though, was that he was going to approach her from behind again and put his hands on her shoulders, more intensely this time.

The first time, she had used her injuries to startle him. But now he had that information, which meant that he would use the possibility of pain as a weapon.

She made herself take a deep breath, followed by a sip of that bubbly concoction. She was slowly coming to the realization that she hated the stuff. It wasn't very good.

She felt him before she saw him. There was a disturbance in the air behind her, and then a hand reached over her right shoulder—barely clearing it—and slammed on the table.

"We get to have drinks together!" Ellis said, sounding joyful. "You showed up!"

Daniella's pulse threatened to reveal just how much he had frightened her. She had to breathe a little to slow it down so that he wouldn't see her rapid pulse in her throat.

That particular quirk of her body had revealed her fear to him once before with disastrous results.

She had to take control of her emotions and the situation, or this entire encounter would be for naught. She slid her chair to the left, and then peered up at him, knowing the move made her seem like an adoring fan.

"I figured we would avoid the food bar," she said. "Too many people at this time of day."

"If only," he said. "No one seems to be around. You'd think, with the ship so jam-packed, everyone would be out and about. But they're scared now after those explosions."

He sounded so matter of fact. Everyone else she had spoken to about the attacks had a tiny thread of fear in their voice when they mentioned it.

Maybe Ellis didn't feel fear. Maybe he had lost whatever contact he had with fear when he had been in prison.

He pulled up the only other chair. It had been on her right, as close to the fountain as she could get it, so that he wouldn't be able to move quickly, but he slid the chair away from the fountain and closer to her.

Their knees nearly touched. She had to suppress a shudder of revulsion. And she had to quell the urge to move as far away from him as possible.

"I guess those attacks spooked everyone," he said, almost as if that baffled him.

She could feel the urge to argue with him, to inform him that some people had *normal* responses to things, unlike him. She'd said something similar to that to him in the past and it had enraged him.

But she was going to take this encounter slowly.

Still, he was giving her an opening. He brought up the attacks right away. But she wasn't going to seem too eager to talk about it, not yet.

"Do you blame them?" she asked.

"Kind of," he said. "I'm here for a vacation. I want to enjoy myself."

Typically self-involved. She supposed she shouldn't have been surprised.

She didn't give him a surprised look, which she kinda felt like he expected. Those words were almost confrontational, and she wasn't ready to confront yet.

"Well," she said as brightly as she could manage, "if you want to enjoy yourself, then you need to try this."

She held up the weird lemony drink concoction and shook it at him.

"I'll order one for you if you like," she said. "My treat."

"Your treat?" he asked. "What, are you made of money these days?"

She ignored that question. Instead, she said, "I bought the whole travel package, so I don't get charged individually for things. I just add items to my tab. If I order something, then it goes into my file."

"You know those all-inclusive things are a scam, right?" He leaned back and crossed his arms. He always had to prove he was superior to her. "The cruise line makes more money off people like you than anyone else."

She already knew how the finances for the trip broke down. Unless she bought every item in the little gift shop or ordered more food than she could eat from the restaurants, the price she paid for all-inclusive would never match what she could have saved by buying each item individually, but she didn't care. She liked the convenience.

Plus she didn't trust the one-to-one pricing. She had learned long ago that some places added taxes and fees and all sorts of surcharges that were never even mentioned in the boilerplate.

But she was trying to charm this guy right now. So she leaned back, fought down her irritation at his assumption that she was too dumb to know how things worked, and trying not to sound too naïve, said, "Oh. I hadn't realized."

A small, superior smile crossed his lips. Then he said, "You were always careless about that stuff, babe."

The *babe* caught her by surprise. It was as if they had a relationship—the kind that involved pet names. She swallowed that, though, and made herself shrug.

"It's too late to change anything now," she said. "So we might as well make use of my overspending." It was very difficult not to put a bit of a charge on that last word. "So, would you like to get a drink?"

She held up the one she hadn't sipped from since he

sat down. The side of the glass had condensation and was starting to feel warm.

His eyes narrowed, making his face even more unpleasant. "You're being suspiciously nice for a woman who said she never wanted to see me again."

There it was. The first attack. She knew that he would just continue to do so, and if she really provoked him, it would get physical before it got productive.

He probably expected her to attack back. That was what she used to do, back when they were studying together at the professor's order. Ellis would attack her and she would feel like she needed to defend herself and her intelligence.

She didn't need to do that any longer.

"Can you blame me?" she asked and not until the words were out of her mouth did she realize that they echoed something she had just said. Not to mention that she sounded defensive, which probably wasn't bad. "I ended up badly hurt."

"I told you I didn't mean to hurt you," he said, a thread of anger underlying his voice. "I *told* you that, and you went to the authorities anyway."

"Well," she said, "I really had no choice, since the neighbors called for help. I felt like I had to cooperate. And then it all just spiraled out of my control. I had no idea how they were going to go after you."

And that part had the benefit of being true. However, a sentence like that had multiple meanings. He didn't need to know that she had no idea what tools the authorities would use to bring him down. He could interpret the sentence as she didn't know they were going to arrest him.

He sucked in his cheeks, then shoved his jaw forward. It was an ugly look, one that made him seem older than he was.

Her heart rate was starting to climb, but she didn't dare do any deep breathing to alleviate it.

"You always were stupid," he said sharply. "And still are, given the fact that you got the all-inclusive package."

Her cheeks heated. That son of a bitch. He was making her angry, maybe deliberately. No one liked being called stupid, and there he was, using that word like a weapon.

"I suppose you got a package that was more sensible," she said, hoping that she wasn't being as sarcastic as she felt.

"You bet I did," he said, "and I was on the cheaper ship, so the money went farther."

"Yeah." She nodded. "I hope they're giving you a discount here."

"They're going to have to give all of us discounts," he said. "Or some kind of compensation." Then he grinned. "And I get the benefit of being with you."

Someone you think is stupid, she would have said in the past. She had to bite the words back.

"Yeah," she said, working to keep a measured tone. Her fingers were gripping that glass much too hard. She had to will herself to loosen them so she didn't break it. "Who could have known this would happen, right?"

He smiled—a real smile this time. It was wide and open and revealed a couple of broken teeth. When he had sucked in his cheeks earlier, he had done so over those teeth, as if they had an energy all their own.

"I knew," he said.

She somehow managed not to smile. She had got him. On the bragging side of things. She had gotten to him.

Maybe. If she continued to let him berate her.

"How could you have known?" she asked.

"Oh, come on," he said. "Anyone with a brain would know. These entertainment systems—cruises, theme rides, holoparties—they don't care about security. They have more holes than that stinky cheese you used to like."

And there it was again, one of those abusive attacks, but subtle, something most people wouldn't notice.

She could feel the hook of the sentence, though. *Swiss cheese isn't stinky. Not like so many other cheeses.*

"Holes?" she asked, and this time she let a bit of fear into her voice. "You mean by booking here, someone could steal my information?"

"Honey," he said, leaning forward. It took all of her strength not to lean away from him. "They can get into your data dot."

A shiver ran through her. She had suspected this, but to hear him say it was something else entirely.

"Oh, my God," she said. "Did you report this?"

He frowned at her, and then got that superior expression again. "Why would I report it? Honey, I designed it."

Got you, you bastard. She had to focus. Too judgmental and she would be in trouble. But she wasn't sure how.

Although he had called her stupid. She could play into that.

"You designed it?" she said. "I'm not sure I understand."

His eyes narrowed again. Somewhere along the way he had become a lot less trusting. "I think maybe you do."

"No," she said. "What would you be designing? And why?"

She almost added, *Surely not because of me.*

"Money," he said. "People pay a lot of money for access."

"Access to…dots?" she asked, as if she had never considered that. In reality, she was one of those people who designed systems to protect the data dots and everything else in a city.

"Sure," he said. "There's a million ways to get that."

"But . . . the attacks," she said. "Surely they got in the way, right?"

His smile grew. It was real again. He was so proud of himself.

"The attacks open the door to the system," he said. "Then you can take what you want."

And he wanted her. She decided to go with that.

"So that's how you found me," she said.

"Don't think this is about you, honey," he said, his smile fading. Apparently, he wanted her to praise him. "It isn't. That was just a lucky accident. You're not that important."

And yet, there he was, talking to her.

"Well, I meant, you know, the court orders . . ."

His cheeks reddened, and his mouth flattened. He shoved himself toward her.

"You think those things will always protect you?" he snarled. "They won't protect you from anything."

He clamped his right hand on her wrist, making tears of pain come to her eyes. He shook that hand a little, splashing the drink. The liquid seeped between his fingers and her skin, warm and sticky.

"I wasn't thinking anything like that," she said, and hoped that Lassiter was going to keep her promise. Because this was going to escalate. "I was just asking a question."

"You were *not*," he said, pulling her toward him. The table hit her in the stomach. "You were reminding me that you humiliated me over and over and over again. You think I would take that forever? You think that you don't deserve to be *punished* for that?"

That was why he was stalking her now? The obsession had turned, just like the therapists said it would. Only Daniella hadn't been around to see it.

She used her free hand to pick up the glass and throw the rest of the liquid in his face.

He screamed, and pulled her closer, swearing at her, using words she hadn't ever heard spoken out loud.

"You think you can hurt me?" he said. "You think you can *take* me? Thanks to you, *sweetheart*, I had to learn how to hurt people and keep it away from any kind of watchful eye."

He slid the hand that was holding her wrist up just enough that he could grab her thumb and pull it back. The pain was sudden and blinding.

And angry-making. She had vowed long ago that she wasn't going to let anyone hurt her again. So she used her hips to shove the table forward, so that it slammed into his crotch. She didn't quite hit the target she wanted, but it still knocked him back. Unfortunately, he took her hand with him, and she fell against the sticky tabletop.

"You think you can win against *me?*" he said. "Because of you, I had to learn how to fight."

He grabbed the back of her head with his other hand, and slammed her face into the tabletop.

"I learned how to hurt people so bad there is no recovery," he said, leaning over her. Her thumb snapped. She both heard it and felt it. A slicing pain went from her thumb all the way up her arm.

She wasn't going to beg him. She wasn't. She had done that before, and it hadn't worked. Nothing worked.

She had tried to get security to come to her rescue, and those people were worthless. And now she was pinned.

"You think I should report those holes in the system?" he said. "You think I should go *whining* to the companies, telling them they made a mistake. You think they'd hire me to *fix* that mistake with my history?"

She couldn't answer him. He was grinding her face into the table. A spoon's sharp edge was digging into her cheek.

"Of course not, but I tried," he said. "I tried real hard, because I was supposed to try. Because they monitor you when you leave, even when you leave under good behavior. And no one would hire me. So I started my own job. And they get to pay."

He had moved to her index finger, pulling it into a position that made it ache.

"Just like you'll get to pay, sweetheart. You're so self-righteous with your little jobs and your degrees. *I bought the whole travel package*." He was mocking her. "And then you offer to order me a drink, like we're friends."

He leaned over her. She shut her eyes. She hoped to hell someone had been listening because her death was going to be for nothing otherwise.

"We're not friends," he said. "You've been trying to destroy my life ever since we met."

And then, suddenly, his head went backwards. His grip on her head loosened, but he raised her injured hand upward, pulling on her arm. The pain was so extreme she saw stars.

He pulled, and then someone took her hand in theirs. A gentle hand went around her back, and helped her up.

Lassiter. She looked concerned.

"Where the hell were you?" Daniella said. Her face was already swelling. The words sounded mushy. He might have broken a bone in her cheek as well.

"We were here," Lassiter said. "We got it."

"And let him do this," Daniella said.

Lassiter nodded. "He was quick. It took only a few seconds to get to you—"

"It felt like days," Daniella snapped. "Years. Not seconds."

"I'm sorry," Lassiter said. "We'll get you to medical."

"Dr. Sylvenia," Daniella said or thought she said. It was almost impossible for her to understand herself as well. "She fixed my hand a few days ago."

And then, a sob started up Daniella's throat, but she swallowed, preventing the sob from coming out.

She had to remember this was her idea. And he hadn't been holding her that long. He couldn't have been. He only said a few things to her.

Before, he had berated her for not showing an interest in him, and this time, he berated her for all the misfortunes in his life.

She scanned the area. He was on the other side of the

water fountain, struggling against two people in security uniforms.

"She goaded me," he was saying. "You have to let me go. She knew that I was here and she trapped me. She wanted me gone. It's your fault that she's even anywhere near me. If you used your system correctly, this would never have happened."

"Bastard," Lassiter said under her breath.

"You have no idea," Daniella said.

The right side of her face ached. It felt like her eye was going to jump out of its socket.

"We got everything," Lassiter said. "His confession, what he'd done, a little on how he had done it. We'll be able to track it all now. You did us a big favor."

Daniella nodded. She didn't feel like talking anymore, but even if she did, she wouldn't say what she was thinking.

Because Lassiter had also done Daniella a favor, no matter how it had ended up. Lassiter had given Daniella a feeling of control.

Before she had let the justice system take over and they had done things their way. Their way was slow and tedious and made her seem like a small chess piece in a much larger game.

Here, though, she was the only reason that Ellis got captured, and she would remain the sole reason that he would go back to prison.

Him and his colleagues.

She hadn't been able to save the others on the boarding bridge, but she would save future people from dying so that someone could break into an entertainment system and steal information.

"Let's get you taken care of," Lassiter said, help her move away from that table. "We owe you, you know."

"Oh, I know," Daniella said, the words round and soft and almost unrecognizable.

And she would take advantage of that. In what kind of ways, she had no idea. Maybe free cruises for life, if Enjoyable Cruises survived this chapter in its history. Maybe a large financial settlement.

Maybe both.

The one thing she wouldn't say, though, was that she had gotten what she wanted.

She had gotten back at Ellis—and he had known it was her.

She hadn't expected that to feel satisfying. Even with the pain. Especially with the pain.

For the first time in her entire life, she felt like she had won.

BUT WAIT, THERE'S MORE!

Want more masterful science fiction?

Go to wmgbooks.com!

Sign up for the Kristine Kathryn Rusch newsletter, and keep up with the latest news, releases and so much more—even the occasional giveaway.

To sign up go to kriswrites.com

Get the latest news and releases from all of WMG's authors and lines, including Kristine Grayson, Kris Nelscott, *Pulphouse Magazine,* and so much more…

To sign up, **go to wmgbooks.com.**

ABOUT THE AUTHOR
KRISTINE KATHRYN RUSCH

Kristine Kathryn Rusch sold more than 35 million books worldwide. She publishes bestselling science fiction and fantasy, award-winning mysteries, acclaimed mainstream fiction, controversial nonfiction, and the occasional romance.

Her novels made bestseller lists around the world and her short fiction appeared in more than twenty best-of-the-year collections. She won more than twenty-five awards for her fiction, including the Hugo, *Le Prix Imaginales*, the *Asimov's* Readers Choice award, and the *Ellery Queen Mystery Magazine* Readers Choice Award.

To find out more about her work, go to her website, kriswrites.com

facebook.com/kristinekathrynruschwriter

patreon.com/kristinekathrynrusch

bookbub.com/authors/kristine-kathryn-rusch